FIVE STAR Review

MARIE REYNARD

PEACE GARDEN
PUBLISHING

FIVE STAR REVIEW

AN ELEMENTAL BONDS NOVELLA

MARIE REYNARD

PEACE GARDEN
PUBLISHING

Cover by Moor Books Design

Illustrations by GetCovers

Beta read by Amy Pittel (Amy Pittel Author Services)

Edited by Kate Wood (Kate Wood Proofreading)

Standard Cover ISBN: 978-1-958002-13-1

Alternative Cover ISBN: 978-1-958002-14-8

First Edition

Published by Peace Garden Publishing, LLC

 Formatted with Vellum

FIVE STAR REVIEW

Gravity, love, and other inevitable falls.

Aiden Lucas is used to a steady stream of discreet packages arriving on his doorstep. It's part and parcel of living with one of the internet's most popular adult toy reviewers, but nothing could have prepared him for the next toy his roommate receives—something that hits a little too close to a secret Aiden has longed to confess for years.

Zayn Parvin has never found a toy worthy of five stars until an anonymous viewer sends him something downright magical—a mysterious model called the Richard Knotz that's not listed anywhere on the internet. The moment he gets his hands, and other parts of his anatomy, on this particular product, he can't stop raving about its special features.

But Zayn is human and shouldn't have been sent merchandise meant exclusively for the supernatural community. His review threatens to expose significantly more than what he usually shows in his videos, and it forces Aiden to make a choice: confess to Zayn, or let a mage wipe Zayn's memory of all things supernatural... including Aiden.

Five Star Review is a 25k steamy best friends to lovers, roommates to mates novella featuring two geeky astronomy majors, some very realistic merchandise, years of pining, a lot of astrophysics homework, and knotting. This stand-alone M/M paranormal romance is set in the Elemental Bonds/MateHub universe and guarantees a HEA for its main couple. It does not contain mpreg.

REC: InZayn Reviews

FabulousFoxxx:
Have you seen this reviewer? He's currently reviewing fantasy toys from some human company. Dragons and tentacles and knots and everything. The noises he makes, oh my god. ASMR level, I swear. I get tingly from his little breathy moans. Could come from the sound alone.

ll_loves_mm:
Ooh, he's cute. His reviews are paywalled?

FabulousFoxxx:
Yeah. Totally worth it though. It's all solo, but he gives the toys a ~thorough~ testing.

KnottyWolf69:
How'd he like the knot?

FabulousFoxxx:
Took him a bit to get it in, but after that, he fucking loved it. Ground on it for a good long while.

KnottyWolf69:
Did he start with it inflated or something?

FabulousFoxxx:

No, it was a human toy. It didn't inflate or anything. I wasn't impressed, but he gave it four stars, and he NEVER gives five stars, so four stars is basically five stars for him.

veryopositive:

Poor human. Can you imagine how blown his mind would be by MateHub toys?

FabulousFoxxx:

Oh man, I wish. Sadly nothing he's said has hinted at him knowing about us.

ll_loves_mm:

That's too bad. I'd absolutely pay to see him ride MateHub's merch. Do you think he could take the Richard Knotz?

FabulousFoxxx:

I guess we'll never find out. But seriously, check out his site! Even if the toys are subpar, his reviews are hot as hell.

veryopositive:

Will check him out! Thanks for the rec!

ONE

NOW

Aiden unlocked the door to his apartment and stepped inside… then nearly did a one-eighty and walked right back out.

The scent of lube and come and satisfaction reached out to greet him. It brushed up against him, wrapped itself around him, and beckoned him toward Zayn's room.

He ignored his wolf's rumble of approval and took a deep, calming breath through his mouth in a desperate attempt to steady himself, to keep from responding to that perfect scent, the one that had been teasing his senses for years. His efforts weren't entirely successful, but they were enough to prevent his dick from busting through his zipper.

After living together for as long as they had, he should have gotten used to the delicious torture of coming home to find Zayn had been filming another review, but he hadn't.

They'd been roommates in the dorms their freshman year of college and had decided to get an apartment together after that. If he'd known the side hustle Zayn was going to start during junior year, he would have… Well, he still would have gotten an apartment with him, no matter how many discreet, unmarked packages arrived at their door. He was a glutton for punishment like that.

Zayn never reviewed products when Aiden was home, but that didn't mean Aiden wasn't aware of every single time he filmed.

Down the hall, the door to Zayn's bedroom opened, and he walked out with a loose-limbed sway that nothing but the best of orgasms could produce. He was fresh from a shower, color high in his cheeks. Was this how he'd look after more mutual activities as well? His golden skin flushed, his brown eyes bright, his black hair no longer meticulously styled. Aiden tried to push the thought away, but it had lived rent-free in his head for so long, it'd gained squatter's rights.

When Zayn saw him standing in the entryway, he grinned. "Oh my god. I'm so glad you're home. I have to show you this."

Before Aiden could ask what, Zayn ducked into his bedroom, then emerged again with a box in one hand and an... impressively large dildo in the other.

Aiden did the only thing he could do. He sat on their couch, grabbed a throw pillow, and placed it casually in his lap. As one did. Just his totally normal, one hundred percent usual way of sitting—clinging to a pillow for dear life.

"I need to tell someone about this. It's *insane*," Zayn said as he plopped onto the couch next to Aiden, a gust of his scent coming with him—sweet, honeyed perfection, a rustle of fall leaves, and beneath that, the maddening knowledge that he was still stretched and ready, still wearing the scent of his orgasm like the headiest of perfumes.

Humans were supposed to have subtle scents, so why

did Zayn's always smack into him like an asteroid hell-bent on causing a mass extinction event? It had taken Aiden a couple days after they'd first met to truly notice, but once he had...

"I've never reviewed anything like this. It's my new favorite toy." Zayn suction-cupped said toy to their coffee table.

Aiden's breath caught as he got a good look at the dildo. He could swear he recognized that... No. He had to be imagining things. It was merely a large dick. A very, *very* realistic one. Uncanny valley level of realistic. But that couldn't be the dick he was thinking of. His extremely human roommate wasn't in possession of *that* piece of merchandise. It was impossible. The only people who could purchase that line of toys knew about the supernatural community, and Zayn did not.

"Right?" Zayn said, misreading Aiden's stunned silence. "It's an absolute monster, but that's not even the craziest part." He flourished the box at Aiden. "It's apparently called the Richard Knotz. And yeah. *Dick knots*. It has an inflatable knot. Like a dog. Plus warming and ejaculating functions. I'm not going to make it ejaculate because it's got force behind it and I don't want to make a mess, but you can definitely feel it."

Oh, fuck.

His extremely human roommate was indeed in possession of something he decidedly should not have been.

Aiden didn't bother to point out that this knot wasn't modeled after a dog. It was a wolf shifter's, and not just any wolf shifter. Richard Knotz was the hottest supernatural porn star in the world; his knotting videos were legendary in their community. But Zayn didn't know any of that.

"You gotta give this thing a try. I swear, I whited out.

Literally lost time. I had to check the recording to be sure, but yep, I came so hard, I zoned out for a solid minute. It's *intense*."

Aiden's mouth opened, but no words came out.

His roommate, his best friend, the love of his life... liked being knotted.

That information had permanently knocked Aiden's brain offline. He might as well drop out of university now. Three and a half years of hard work be damned, there was no finishing his senior thesis after that revelation.

"Umm..." he managed to say before Zayn reached out and started rolling the lifelike foreskin down, then up to cover the head, before retracting it again. Aiden held back a distressed whimper and clutched his pillow tighter.

"Look at how the foreskin moves. I've reviewed dildos with foreskin before, but none of them felt like this. The way it glides must be new technology. It's so silky. I bet I can use this for docking. There's enough here, and I've been wanting to try that." As if to prove his point, he rolled it forward with one hand, then ran two fingers of the other along the inside.

It was official. Aiden had entered his own personal hell. That was the only rational explanation for what was happening here. He'd pissed off the powers that be, and now they were punishing him by making him watch Zayn gently trail his fingers over the head of a magically created dildo, teasing the edge of its foreskin.

Zayn slowed the motion as he glanced at Aiden. He wet his lips. "...Do you have...?" He retracted the foreskin another time, his thumb swiping over the now-exposed head.

"Yeah," Aiden said, though the word was strangled. He

very much did have, and if Zayn wanted to try docking, he didn't need a toy to do it. He cleared his throat. "So. Where did you get that?"

There was no way Zayn had access to the shop that sold it. MateHub, the supernatural community's best porn site, operated on a strict 'if you know, you know' basis. And as much as Aiden wished otherwise, Zayn didn't know.

"One of my viewers sent it anonymously to my PO box, but I have no idea where they got it from. I can't find anything about it online." He stopped giving the toy a handjob and picked up the box. "This says it's from the MateHub Shifter Line. I searched for that. Nothing came up. But this has to be a bestseller. I mean, watch this."

He pulled a remote out of the box and pressed a button marked with an up arrow. On their coffee table, the Richard Knotz started to live up to its name. Its knot gradually expanded with every press.

"There must be some kind of mechanism inside," Zayn said. "But I can't figure it out. And it's so quiet. Almost like magic."

Not *almost*. Aiden smelled the enchantments that had been placed on it, the spells the MateHub mages used to make it throb and expand the same way a real knot would.

"I mean, I've reviewed knotting dildos before. Those videos get the most views—them and all the fantasy-creature-inspired toys—and I see an increase in payments on my 'Just the Tip' button whenever I post one. But this..." He wrapped a hand around the sizable knot. "It's completely different. You can feel it pulse inside you. Here, touch it."

"I'm... good? Thanks?" Aiden's voice came out embarrassingly high-pitched.

"Oh, don't worry. I cleaned it."

That much was clear from the scent and wasn't even ranking on Aiden's current list of concerns.

His biggest worry at the moment was also the least important. He knew that, but it was hard not to develop a complex. There were many reasons Richard Knotz was a legend, and the largest was currently sticking straight up from their coffee table.

Did Zayn always want something that... girthy? That long? Aiden wasn't small himself, but in comparison...

"It's a bit, uh..."

"Yeah," Zayn agreed, somehow guessing what Aiden was trying to say. "It really is. I honestly didn't make it to level-ten inflation. I mean, don't get me wrong, I'll be giving it another go, but I was hoping they had a size smaller. A few inches shorter, a little less girth, and it'd be perfect. Then I'd get to level ten for sure." He let out a huff. "But if they have other sizes or products, I can't find *anything*. So I don't know what to do. I can't put up a review without a link to the product. My viewers are going to want their own, and I'd be missing out on affiliate income."

Aiden seized on that.

"Maybe it's a prototype? Someone might have sent you an early version, but they're not quite ready to launch, so their shop isn't online yet. Wait a few days and check again."

That wasn't it, but it would give Aiden time to figure out what the hell he should do about this.

Zayn slumped against the couch. "You're probably right." He stared at the toy for a beat before glancing at Aiden again. "Ever wonder what it'd be like if humans could do something like that?"

"Uh. No. Can't say I have." It wasn't a lie. He never

thought about *humans* having knots. Certain humans getting knotted, on the other hand...

"I suppose." Zayn sighed. "It feels amazing though."

Zayn wanted to be knotted for real. This was knowledge Aiden was never going to recover from.

"But seriously," Zayn said. "You've gotta get one of these."

I already have one, Aiden thought. Okay, not yet, but he could. With the right person.

"At least I have Mr. Knotz to keep me company now," Zayn continued. "He and I will be getting to know each other real well."

Aiden wanted to growl at a sex toy. He wanted to storm his way into the MateHub headquarters and demand Richard Knotz keep his merchandise away from his ma— *room*mate.

But that was his wolf talking, not a logical response. No one in their right mind got jealous of a dildo. He wasn't thinking about how it would be such a shame if it had an accidental run-in with their garbage disposal. A sane, well-adjusted shifter wouldn't do that. Besides, the thought alone had him wishing for something more protective than a pillow to cover his dick. He'd never be able to go through with it; the toy was too realistic.

Zayn sighed again, then straightened up. "Did you finish the Astro Techniques homework?"

Aiden nodded, relieved they were changing the subject to more explored space. He carefully avoided looking at their coffee table as he answered. "Yeah, that last photometric analysis was killer."

"What did you do with the two outliers?"

"Dropped the one that appeared to be a measurement

error and kept the second, since it seemed like a genuine extreme value. You?"

"Same." Zayn grinned at him. "Ready for our overnight trip to the observatory next week?"

"Of course," Aiden said. They had research to do, but even if they didn't, he still wouldn't miss it for all the galaxies in the universe.

TWO

THEN

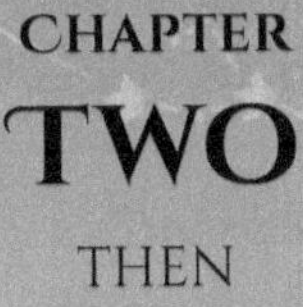

September, Freshman Year

When Zayn arrived at his new dorm room, he found the door propped open. He stopped in the doorway and blinked at the sight that greeted him.

A guy was in there already, bent over, using incorrect lifting form as he set down a box. Not that Zayn could formulate a complaint when it meant he was getting the perfect view of some excellent musculature in sweatpants.

The guy seemed to be trying to fit the box under the bed on the right, but it was a fraction of an inch too tall. Instead of giving up, he simply lifted the side of the bed about a foot off the floor with one hand and no apparent effort, slid the box under it with the other, then casually set the bed back down.

Zayn blinked harder. There was no way he'd just seen that. Not even with how impressive this guy's arms were.

The guy spun around, looking startled to find Zayn

standing there, then grinned, his wide smile shining with the absolute magnitude of a blue supergiant, and Zayn forgot everything he knew about weight and force and leverage and logic.

"Hey! Are you Zayn Parvin?"

Zayn shook his head frantically. "Wrong room." It came out as a high-pitched squeak, and he would have been embarrassed about that, but he was too busy turning on his heel to escape.

This could not be his roommate. He'd gotten an email the day before explaining that there'd been an administrative error regarding his room assignment, and the computer science major he'd been messaging for the last month would, in fact, not be rooming with him. Instead, he'd be living with an Aiden Lucas, major unknown, last-minute attempt to contact so far unanswered. Googling him hadn't produced any useful information either.

But this couldn't be Aiden Lucas. The college wouldn't do that to him. Raid his fantasies and assign him a roommate who looked like this—all tall and muscular, with sun-kissed skin and golden blond hair, the poster boy cliché of a popular high school quarterback, the football team captain with a smile that threatened to vaporize Zayn on impact.

There must have been a mistake. He'd likely have to go to an office somewhere and fill out a bunch of forms to get this straightened out, because he couldn't live with someone this attractive for an entire year without making a complete fool of himself.

Except his exit was foiled by his parents' arrival. His mother's gaze caught on Hopefully-Not-Aiden. "Oh, are you Zayn's roommate?" she asked as she hustled Zayn inside.

The guy's brow furrowed in confusion. "He said he's not in this room."

Zayn's mother peeked her head out of the door to double-check the number. "No. This is the room Zayn's supposed to be in."

Well, there went his chance to escape nine months of pretending he wasn't drooling over his plasma-hot roommate. He should have tried harder to convince his parents he didn't need any help moving.

His mother set her box on the desk, then his father did the same.

"Aiden." The guy extended a hand, and they exchanged greetings.

Zayn edged over to shake his hand as well. "Zayn," he said, then swallowed in a way he hoped wasn't audible to every single person in the building. Did Aiden's hand have to be so warm and big?

"Is your family here to help you move in?" his mother asked, but Aiden shook his head.

"No, ma'am, I'm by myself today. I didn't have that much stuff, and it's a couple days' drive, so I didn't want to drag everybody down here with me."

"Ah, a bit of a lone wolf, are you?"

An expression of sheer panic crossed Aiden's face. "What? No. I'm not a wolf, lone or otherwise."

"Well," she said with a laugh. "In that case, we'll help you."

Aiden hesitated, like he was searching for a polite way to say no, but then he grinned that bright, easy smile. "Thank you. That's very nice of you to offer."

Between the four of them, they finished unpacking both cars in no time, and then Zayn's mother was bundling them off to a nearby restaurant for an early dinner, refusing to take no for an answer when Aiden tried to insist he could just use his cafeteria meal plan.

Given his luck for the day, Zayn wasn't surprised to find himself on the same side of the booth as Aiden. The booth wasn't small, but the only thing he could focus on was the space between them, how close they were sitting, how Aiden seemed to possess a special brand of gravity that was trying to pull Zayn closer to him still.

After the waitress had taken their order, Zayn's mother looked at Aiden. "What are you majoring in?"

Aiden immediately sat up straighter, energy radiating from him. "Astronomy."

Zayn's eyebrows rose. He must have heard that wrong. Aiden, with his muscles and his height and his arms and his everything, was *not* an astronomy major.

"Oh, that's lovely," his mother said. "Zayn is too."

Aiden turned toward him, and Zayn was going to have to develop an entirely new classification system for luminosity, because Morgan and Keenan had not taken into account a smile like Aiden's when they developed theirs.

"You're an astronomy major? Nice! My high school was super rural, so I've had to study as much as I can on my own, but I'm so excited. When are you taking Astronomy Lab this term? Tuesday? Mine's on Tuesdays. Do you think they'll cover detecting exoplanets? I know it's not really introductory material, but exoplanets are so cool. Even if we only got to analyze simulated light curves to identify exoplanet candidates, it'd be *amazing*."

Oh god. Aiden was a big geek. A big smart geek who knew about astronomy. No. This was not okay. It was one thing when he was just gorgeous, but now he was talking about exoplanets with his eyes glittering like the stars on a moonless night in a dark-sky location. Zayn didn't have the mental fortitude to deal with this.

He managed to nod. "I'd love it if they covered microlensing, but I think that won't happen until maybe third year. We'll have to get through general relativity first."

"You're probably right. Which are you looking forward to learning more, the transit method or the radial velocity method? Ooh, or transit spectroscopy? I mean, obviously the answer is 'all of them,' but I can't wait to study the transit method. It's been used to detect so many planets, and it'll be fascinating to learn how to calculate a planet's size and orbital distance."

What? No. Hot or not, Zayn needed to make sure Aiden knew how ridiculous he was being. "The follow-up studies are going to be way more interesting. Like using transit spectroscopy to analyze the composition of a planet's atmosphere? How cool will it be to learn to detect signs of potential habitability?"

"Yeah, it's gonna be *awesome*."

Damn right it was.

Somewhere between the finer details about dependence on specific instrument capabilities and contributions to the overall understanding of exoplanetary population, their food arrived.

Zayn realized both his parents had the same indulgent, if completely baffled, smiles on their faces that they always got when he talked about astronomy, but he couldn't bring himself to care. For the first time in his life, he had someone to talk to in person who truly understood. Even if Aiden had some mistaken priorities when it came to learning exoplanet detection and characterization techniques. Clearly, using radial velocity to help characterize a planet's orbit would be more fun than observing periodic dips in a star's brightness with the transit method. But that was forgivable when Aiden seemed so passionate about detecting Earth-sized planets in habitable zones.

And if, after his parents dropped them off at their dorm, they spent the rest of the night talking about the limitations of ground-based observatories instead of unpacking, well, he'd survive a day or two without putting his underwear and socks in a drawer.

THREE

Aiden grabbed his laptop and settled onto his bed. He was going to regret this. Every time he watched Zayn's reviews, he regretted it, and he'd seen more of them than he wanted to admit.

Okay, fine. He'd watched *all* of them, and he didn't regret it nearly as much as he should have. But if he were a good person with morals, he absolutely would regret what he was about to do.

If he had fewer morals, he'd claim his actions were solely to assess the damage this situation could cause. Not that anyone would believe him.

Zayn's blog, InZayn Reviews, was one of the most popular sex toy review sites on the internet, for reasons Aiden completely understood. Zayn had confessed its existence to him toward the beginning of their junior year—a revelation that had both blindsided Aiden and sent him running for his laptop and credit card. Before that, he'd assumed Zayn simply liked to... indulge himself. Frequently. He hadn't realized there'd be accompanying videos for a low monthly fee.

He'd never told Zayn he'd joined the paywalled members-only area that had access to his video reviews, not just the publicly available write-ups, or that his blog was a near-nightly visit.

While Zayn's videos were thankfully solo and relatively tame, they were better than every single scene Aiden had ever watched on MateHub.

Sending up a silent apology for violating the sanctity of their shared cloud drive, he opened Zayn's personal folder and made a quick copy of the raw video Zayn had uploaded. He'd never done this before; he'd always waited for the reviews to be posted to Zayn's site, even if he could smell exactly when Zayn had been filming. But excuses aside, he needed to know how bad this was.

That didn't mean he wouldn't also be using it to torture himself. Repeatedly. Starting now.

Already knowing this would be the end of him, he clicked on the file and braced himself for what he was about to watch. All twenty minutes of it. Zayn's longest review ever. Appropriate, given the toy he was reviewing.

He did his best to ignore the shiver of arousal that ran through him as the video began to play.

On screen, Zayn was in his bedroom, wearing a blue bathrobe that he'd be losing shortly.

"I've got something special for you today. This is a request from one of you, and oh boy, whoever you are, Anon, I'd be confessing my love to you, but I'm afraid this thing you sent me has stolen my heart. And I haven't even tested it out yet." Zayn grinned at the camera, and Aiden sighed, painfully aware he sounded like a lovesick puppy.

The lights behind the camera reflected in Zayn's dark, expressive eyes and emphasized his high cheekbones, somehow making his tan skin appear even warmer and more alluring than usual. What Aiden wouldn't give to touch him in the ways he'd been fantasizing about for years.

"I'm in the process of tracking down the details on this, but once I do, I'll put it in the description. I have a feeling you'll want your own."

He held up the toy. "Let me introduce you to Mr. Richard Knotz. He is a girthy specimen. I have to admit, he's a bit of an intimidating beast, but I can't wait to try him out. So let's get to another InZayn review. Richard Knotz edition." He snorted. "Such a ridiculous name.

"This is the most realistic dildo I have ever seen or felt. You know those porn videos where someone switches places with a toy, like the person using it isn't going to notice that suddenly it's become significantly more lifelike? Well, if they were using Mr. Knotz here, I would understand. This feels real, with a nice weight to it. Blindfold me and put this in my hand, and the only thing that would give me pause is its massive size. Regardless of what most of you are probably claiming on your Grindr profiles, statistically speaking, the average guy is not packing anything close to this monster."

He ran through its features one by one, first playing with the foreskin the same way he'd done in the living room, then fondling its balls and explaining it would come with the touch of a button.

"I do like it when my men can come on command," he said with a wink.

Then he got into its wildest function, inflating its knot to level ten, his eyes going wide as he stared at it. "Not gonna lie, I'm a little unsure about that. But we'll give it a try."

Aiden winced. Fuck, fuck, *fuck*. This should not have

been sent to Zayn. They'd be in so much trouble if this review got posted. Whoever did this was a moron, but at the same time, Aiden couldn't blame them. He also wanted to see Zayn get knotted, and the sad human attempts at knotting toys Zayn had reviewed in the past didn't count.

Though, if he were being honest about what he wanted, it wouldn't be MateHub's finest merchandise knotting Zayn.

Zayn stood and slipped off his robe. The soft material slid down his arms to reveal his naked body, his half-hard cock, and Aiden prayed to any powers listening for his sanity to survive this, though he doubted any being, divine or otherwise, could help on that front.

"Its suction cup is nice and strong." Zayn stuck it onto the sturdy wooden chair he used whenever he reviewed products like this, then gave it a few firm tugs to prove his point. "There shouldn't be any issues if you get vigorous as you ride it."

He ran lubed fingers over the toy, slicking it up, then glanced at the camera again. "I'm stretched and ready to go. Let's see if this bad boy feels as good in me as it does in my hand."

Watching Zayn line himself up with a firm grip around the shaft, then slowly sink onto the dildo, was a maddening exercise as always, but the knowledge of how this was going to be different had Aiden's stomach clenching in anticipation.

Zayn shifted his hips, taking the toy in with shallow thrusts, its thick length stretching him open a little more each time he bore down.

Aiden's dick throbbed at the idea of it being him instead; his wolf rumbled its approval. He cupped himself through his pants and gave himself a squeeze.

Yes, he was a horrible person, but god, Zayn was hot.

Zayn gasped softly. "Oh, this is nice, but make sure you stretch well before you give it a go." He let out a breathy moan, his eyelids fluttering and his right hand jerking himself to full hardness with the rhythm he used most often, the one Aiden had committed to memory months ago.

Aiden unzipped his pants and pulled himself out, rolling his foreskin back like Zayn had done to the toy.

"Oh, that's good," Zayn said as he took the last inch in and was fully seated. "It's nice and firm with some give to it. Definitely on the large side, but you already knew that. Any size queens out there, you need this."

He started to move, building up speed until he was bouncing on it, moaning, his thighs straining with effort, and Aiden stroked himself in time. For a moment, he thought Zayn might not get to testing out the knot, but then Zayn seemed to catch himself. He laughed breathlessly.

"Almost got carried away. I cannot stress enough how realistic it feels. I could get off on this alone, no extra features necessary. But that's not why we're here, is it?" He snickered. "*Knot.* Actually, you're going to think I sound crazy, and maybe this thing is making me lose my mind, but I swear its base is throbbing, like the knot is waiting to expand. So let's do that."

He grabbed the remote and held it up for the camera. "Level one, what've you got?"

Aiden's gaze latched onto the toy as Zayn hit the up button and raised and lowered himself. There was the slightest of swells at its base.

"Hmm, with as big as this is, I can't feel it that much. So moving on to level two."

This time, when he pulled off, the knot was easier to see. Zayn bounced on it a few times. "Alright, that I notice more. Yeah, there's a nice little extra stretch to that. Not enough to cause any true resistance, but enough to feel it. Let's try three. Ooh, three tugs on my rim, but damn, that feels good. I need to apply more pressure to get it in and out. Mmm. Yeah. I like that."

Aiden gripped the base of his dick with one hand while he jerked himself with the other, imagining his knot throbbing and expanding inside Zayn.

With the speed he was riding that dildo, Zayn looked like he might lose himself again, but once more, he remembered what he was supposed to be doing.

"Okay, fuck. I can't get distracted. I've got a review to film here. What will level four do? Ooh. Yeah, four. Four catches. It requires some bearing down, but it feels amazing. This is an order of magnitude better than the other knotting toys I've reviewed. With how this gradually expands, you can build up to it."

As if to make his case, he popped the knot in and out a few times, and Aiden bit his lip to keep himself from whimpering. How would it feel to have Zayn's tight ass wrapped around his knot? To stretch him open more and more with each thrust until they were tied together.

The idea alone almost had his wolf howling.

"Yeah," Zayn said, his voice raspy with pleasure, "spoiler alert so it doesn't shock you too much when it happens. This is getting five stars from me. And speaking of five. Let's go. Oh, *oh*. Okay. Five doesn't want to come out, but I could force it if I needed to. It pulls quite a bit when I try to lift off it, and oh god... the way it's stretching my rim. So good. And when I'm sitting fully on it, it's pressed right against my prostate. What if I..."

He rotated his hips and moaned, making Aiden buck into his hand. Shit. The sounds that came out of his mouth. Aiden wanted to hear them in person, to have Zayn moan in his ear.

"Oh fuck. Grinding on this thing is beyond pleasurable. If you're a fan of prostate stimulation, this will be a new favorite for you. Let's try six."

The moment he clicked the button, he groaned, long and low, then he stilled, panting. He didn't say a word. Instead, his shaky fingers hit the button another time and brought the knot to level seven.

His eyes rolled back, and he panted as he ground on the dildo. "Oh. This is... this is..."

Aiden had never seen Zayn speechless during a review. He was always able to articulate what he was feeling and if he liked it. There was no question about whether or not he liked this. His loss of words spoke volumes, too caught up in the sensations it was bringing him for anything more than that.

Aiden thrust up into his fist, his pleasure tied with Zayn's, getting closer as Zayn did.

"Fuck," Zayn said. "Sorry, guys. This is just really good."

He lifted up the remote, his hand shaking to the point it was a wonder he managed to press the button at all, but when he did, he keened, throwing back his head and writhing on the toy, his other hand stroking his dick with an almost frantic rhythm. He didn't always jerk himself to completion in these reviews, especially if he wasn't enjoying the product. But with this, it was like he couldn't help himself.

It was only a minute before his orgasm hit him as he moaned, and that was another first. He'd come on camera before, but never hard enough to paint his chest with it.

Aiden came with him, spilling over his fingers, his vision blacking out at the edges, but he forced his eyes to stay open and locked on the screen.

He wanted to lick the come off Zayn's skin, to follow its path up to his neck, to sink his teeth in, to bite, to claim. To see if Zayn would come even harder on a real knot. His canines ached with the urge to do just that.

Zayn hung there, panting, eyelids pressed shut. He hadn't lied. It was a solid minute of him clearly out of it, his hips still making the occasional aborted movement.

Finally, he blinked back to reality. "Sorry. Got carried away again. Guess I didn't reach level ten after all. But let's try out this other feature."

His fingers left smudges of come on the remote as he pressed the button to make it ejaculate. He moaned—a satisfied, husky sound that had Aiden's dick trying desperately to get hard again.

"Ooh, nice. You can feel it. Multiple spurts, and the dildo pulses with each one. Yeah. If you've never had someone come in you, this is the next best thing." He breathed in, then sighed. "I kind of want to keep this in me longer, but let's deflate it."

Well fuck. All Aiden could imagine was them lying together, tied together, his arms wrapped around Zayn, waiting for him to recover, then grinding into him and making him come again. Keeping him filled and sated for as long as he wanted.

Zayn hit the down arrow twice to deflate the knot to level six, and the fake come began to leak out onto the toy's balls. "Ah. I'm already missing the fullness. The instructions said they recommend trying to pull it out when it's half-inflated for the total 'Richard Knotz experience,' whatever that means. But let's give that a try, and let's get you some ASMR as I do."

He grabbed the mic that had been out of frame and lowered it.

"Okay, here goes. Back to level five."

There was a slick pop and a squelch as he lifted off the toy. Fake come gushed out of Zayn, leaving him messy and stretched, his legs shaky, just like Richard Knotz left all his co-stars in his knotting scenes.

"Oh, that's... Fuck. That was more than the average load, but I can't say I didn't like it."

Zayn glanced down and laughed at the absolute mess that was his chair, then grinned sheepishly. "We'll have to end it here today. I've got some serious cleanup to do. But, final rating? Five stars. Honestly, five doesn't seem to be enough for Mr. Knotz. I highly recommend the ride he'll give you. He's going into heavy rotation for me. Let me know if you want me to give reaching level ten another go."

Waving one sticky hand, he leaned forward and turned the camera off with his other. The last frames showed him bringing his fingers up to lick them clean, the video cutting off right before he slipped them into his mouth.

Aiden groaned and flopped back onto his bed.

That had been the hottest review Zayn had ever filmed. It was somehow exactly what Aiden had been afraid of and also exactly what he'd wanted to see.

Fine, not *exactly*. There wouldn't be any screens or cameras involved in his ideal scenario.

He'd be lying if he said he'd never been curious to know what Zayn would think of MateHub's merchandise. Part of him wondered if he'd ordered the toy for Zayn in a fugue state, but he hadn't. He wasn't that big of a masochist.

If this review were posted, everyone in the comments would agree they wanted a follow-up video of him trying to get to level ten. They'd offer him their firstborn, grovel at his feet, bend over and let him ream their ass—whatever he demanded.

Aiden wasn't sure he could take a repeat, but he'd be right there with them.

He wasn't going to be able to look Zayn in the eye after this. Sure, he'd watched all his reviews, but none had hit this close to home. He already fantasized about Zayn more than he should, but having the visual of him blissed out on a knot only added fuel to the fire.

As he lay on his bed in a state of post-nut shame and clarity, Aiden sighed, staring at the ceiling.

Humans were complicated. Even if he got his alpha's permission to tell Zayn, how would he bring up the subject of being a wolf shifter to a human? Especially in a way that wouldn't end with Zayn either thinking he was certifiable or running for the hills.

"Hey, roomie who I've been lusting after for years, want to know why I usually have a 'family dinner' on the full moon? Why your scent drives me crazy? Why, if my alpha would allow it, I could give you the real version of what you experienced with that toy?"

Not that it mattered; their time together was likely nearing an end. They'd applied to the same grad schools, but if they didn't get into the same program, they'd be moving who-knew-where. Which left Aiden counting down the days until they didn't have the excuse of university to keep them in each other's orbit. Plus, he'd eventually need to return to his pack.

And no matter what his wolf told him, Zayn wasn't part of it.

When he'd moved into the dorms, Aiden had brought a large blanket with him. It had been wrapped up tight in a box he'd kept tucked under his bed. Wolf shifters didn't always react well to being away from their pack for extended periods, and the blanket had been in case his wolf needed their scent to help it settle into college life. He hadn't taken it out once; Zayn's scent in the air was all he needed for their dorm room to smell like home.

But he'd never let himself think he could have Zayn in reality. From a young age, it'd been drilled into him that they had to hide their existence. Humans would freak out if they discovered the supernatural. Wolf shifters never told humans about themselves—not without a valid reason. And as much as he respected his alpha, he doubted Grant would think 'I've been fantasizing about biting and knotting Zayn since the first week of my freshman year' would be considered valid. Though his wolf whined and protested the thought of not doing that.

He wanted to believe Zayn would be fine with it, but he couldn't be sure, and he couldn't take rejection over what he was. Not from Zayn. He'd rather have Zayn as a friend than have to call magical law enforcement to wipe his memories because he'd freaked out and was threatening to expose supernatural creatures to the world. He didn't think Zayn would do that, but he'd heard stories about humans doing similar things before.

That was all logical and reasonable, but damn if he wasn't thinking about showing Zayn some of the knotting videos on MateHub to see his reaction. Maybe he could pretend it was CGI or some kind of unique cock sleeve. But it was too risky.

Which brought him back to the real problem. No human should have MateHub merchandise. It was too dangerous. If this video got out, people would have questions.

He needed to do something about it. He just didn't know what.

FOUR

THEN

September, Freshman Year

"I'm so psyched we're observing deep-sky objects this term," Zayn said as he and Aiden exited their first Astronomy Lab. "I've only been able to convince my parents to bring me to a dark-sky location three times. But last year, for my birthday, they got me a new telescope and took me to Death Valley, and I saw the central bulge of the Andromeda Galaxy so much brighter than I'd ever seen it before. I could even make out the inner part of the disk surrounding it."

"Nice. What size is your aperture?"

"Just six inches with a focal ratio of f-eight. I wish it were bigger."

Aiden's expression became mischievous. "Size isn't the most important factor. I mean, a twelve-inch aperture doesn't always have the best performance."

Feeling daring, Zayn asked, "Is that so?"

"Yeah. Quality of optics and design over size any day.

Especially if you have the skill and experience to handle it right.”

“So what size is yours?”

“Eight inches.” Aiden’s little smirk was doing things to Zayn’s insides.

Oh god. Were they flirting? Was this flirting? It kind of felt like flirting.

Aiden pulled up short and looked around. For a second, he seemed to be sniffing the air, which was weird, then his gaze landed on a guy walking through the quad.

“Hold that thought,” Aiden said. “I’ll be right back.”

Before Zayn could respond, Aiden was jogging after the guy. The stunningly pretty guy, his black hair contrasting with skin as pale as porcelain in the evening light. There was something about him that made the hair on Zayn’s neck want to stand on end, that made him feel like he should back away slowly so as not to draw attention to himself. But that was ridiculous. The guy was simply walking across campus; he wasn’t some apex predator on the hunt for prey.

When Aiden bounded up to him, the guy stopped and gave Aiden a thorough once over. His eyebrow quirked, he asked a question that had Aiden nodding, almost bouncing on his feet.

The guy shot him a skeptical look as he gestured between them, but Aiden shook his head and smiled that beautiful, bright smile of his. Whatever he said in return, it had a slow grin spreading across the guy’s face. He took out his phone, and they exchanged numbers.

Zayn sighed. Ah. So *this* was what flirting felt like.

He couldn’t be too disappointed though. From the moment they’d met, he’d known Aiden was so far out of his league, they didn’t even exist in the same galaxy. Nothing was going to happen between them, and Zayn had to admit Aiden and this guy would make a gorgeous couple. Dwelling on impossibilities was an illogical waste of time.

But then Aiden was at his side again. "Sorry about that. Yeah, I can't wait to get a good look at the Pleiades star cluster when it rises early enough. This year is going to be awesome."

He was right, Zayn decided. While he might not be Aiden's type, it was fine. He finally had a friend who knew what gravitational lensing was, and who needed anything more than that?

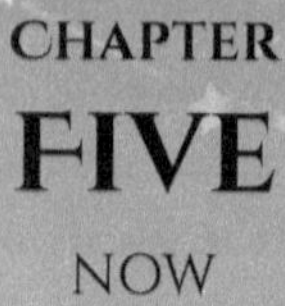

Bram started laughing the moment he opened the door to let Aiden in. "That shell-shocked expression can only mean one thing. The human just posted a new review."

"No, this is so much worse," Aiden said as he stepped inside, then threw himself down onto Bram's couch.

"That bad? Need a drink?"

"Yes, please, but not what you're drinking."

Bram scoffed. "I'm not wasting perfectly good blood on you."

Aiden never would have predicted that his best friend, aside from Zayn, would be a vampire. He hadn't been around one before. Wolf shifters and vampires tended to avoid each other whenever possible, but there was a natural camaraderie to being part of the small handful of supernaturals at their university. It was nice to have someone who knew what he was and understood the issues he had, even if their particular issues were never quite the same. He'd been surprised by how well they got along, though it had taken time to get used to the scent of a vampire. Bram still smelled a bit like death to him, but Aiden couldn't hold that against him.

Bram grabbed Aiden a beer and sat on the other end of the couch. "What's up? Did the human get another boyfriend?"

Thankfully, no. Zayn didn't date or hook up often anymore, but when he did, it always killed Aiden a little inside. Their sophomore year had been particularly rough. Zayn had been experimenting, but that phase had mostly passed.

Right now, a boyfriend might have been easier to deal with.

"One of his viewers sent him a package to review. And I mean that literally. It was the Richard Knotz merch."

Bram's eyes widened. "Seriously? Oh shit, dude. That's not coo—Wait. Did he review it? Holy shit. Did he post it on his site?" He grabbed for his phone, and Aiden groaned.

"Yes, yes, and not yet."

Bram sagged against the couch and let out a sigh of relief. "Oh thank god. I was imagining a thousand-plus humans watching him review that thing." He glanced at Aiden. "But you saw it?"

"Yeah. He... uh... enjoyed it."

"Same, man. Can't blame him. Richard's merch is a work of art. Have you tried it? It's amazing. But who was the dumbass who sent it to him?"

"Someone with access to MateHub, obviously. He gets higher views when he reviews fantasy dildos, so I've always suspected at least a few supernatural types had joined his site."

"Hold on. Let me check something." Bram scrolled on his phone as Aiden sipped his beer.

"Oh, here we go. I rarely check the Off Topic board on

the MateHub forum. I mean, I'm there for the MateHub stars. Who'd want to talk about anything else? But there's a thread about him, started a few months ago. Some of the forum members love his reviews."

He passed over his phone so Aiden could scroll through the thread. Yep, Zayn might not know about the supernatural community, but at least one corner of the supernatural community knew about him. Fuck.

He was about to hand the phone back when Bram's username caught his eye. "Bram... Stroker?"

"I've been told it was a stroke of genius." Bram shrugged.

"It's a stroke of something, alright."

"I can't believe some idiot sent him Richard's merch. But damn, can you imagine him reviewing all of MateHub's merch? The entire Shifter Line. Richard's is the best, of course, but ooh, I wonder how he'd feel about the shark shifters. Or there are some thick bear shifter toys. He might like those."

Aiden growled before he could stop himself, and Bram raised an eyebrow at him.

"Really, dude? I've never seen you get truly growly and possessive over him, even when he has a boyfriend. The Richard Knotz is where you draw the line?"

It was a dumb reaction, but he was still jealous of a goddamn toy. "It's one thing when he's reviewing fake fantasy tentacle dildos, but MateHub's merch is modeled after real guys, and I do not measure up."

Bram snorted. "Nobody measures up to Richard. He's a legend for a reason." He cocked his head. "If Zayn did reviews for MateHub, do you think he'd get to meet him?"

"He can't do reviews for MateHub, you know that."

"And you know you have to report this, right? MateHub has an emergency contact number in case a human finds out about the site. I bet it's the same for their toys."

Aiden sighed. "I know. I just... He smells so good."

Bram looked over at him with a soft expression. "You thought this might be your chance to tell him?"

"It's stupid, right? The fact that I've been mooning over him for more than three years."

"Nah. It'd be stupid if you waited another three."

"What if he freaks out?"

"Then he wasn't good enough for you in the first place."

"He's more than good enough for me."

"Then you shouldn't have to worry about him freaking out. But if you aren't going to tell him, you need to contact MateHub. *Before* he posts that video."

Aiden grimaced. "I'll call them tonight."

Aiden stared at the MateHub contact page and its giant 'In Case of Emergencies*' phone number listed right at the top.

The asterisk led to a note farther down the page that said, "Needing to get railed by any or all of our stars does not constitute an emergency."

He dialed the number.

"MateHub Studios. How may I help you?" a pleasant customer service voice said after it connected.

"Um, I'm not sure if I should contact you about this, or your store, or who, but uh, my roommate is human, and..." He trailed off.

"Did he see the site, sir?" the lady on the phone asked.

"No. Uh. He somehow got a MateHub toy and wants to post a video of him using it on the internet. The *human* internet. For people to watch. And that seems like a bad idea."

"It's okay," she said, her tone soothing. "This has happened before. There are protections and protocols in place. It was part of the agreement the mages signed with us before making the things. They included safety measures in case some unknowing human got their hands, or other parts of their anatomy, on one. He'll never be able to post that video anywhere other than MateHub or OnlyMates. It'll corrupt itself if he tries."

Well, that was terrifying. How did they monitor that?

"Can we send a mage to take care of the situation?"

Aiden's stomach dropped. "What do you mean by '*take care of*?'"

"Not like that. We need to make sure he won't expose us. Our mage will ask him a few questions to assess the situation and go from there. Most of the time, that requires a memory spell or blood oath of secrecy. Neither will harm the human."

"Okay. I suppose." He gave her their address, and she told him a mage would be there the following evening.

"In the meantime, would you be able to get the toy back from him?"

"He seems... quite fond of it. I don't think he'll give it up without a fight."

The lady laughed. "That's usually how it goes. Which model is it?"

"The Richard Knotz model."

"That's definitely a fan favorite. Size queens love it."

Aiden wanted to protest that Zayn wasn't a size queen, but that didn't seem like information she needed to know.

"Don't worry. We've got this covered. Our mage will handle it."

"Okay, thank you," he said, then stared at his phone for a good minute after he'd hung up, hoping he'd done the right thing.

December, Freshman Year

College was awesome, Zayn thought as he walked to his dorm room. He hadn't been a fan of high school, definitely would not recommend.

Well, okay, he'd recommend it, but only in the same way he'd recommend regular dental cleanings. Necessary, not enjoyable. The educational equivalent of standing in line at the DMV. Maddening at the time, but required if you wanted to get to the fun destinations further down the road.

Because college? College was *fun*. And he hadn't even gotten to the truly fun classes yet. Those wouldn't happen for another year or two, but that didn't mean he couldn't enjoy Calculus for Science or Physics or Intro to Astronomy, even if that last one was a bit easy and too many non-astronomy majors took it. Plus there were the clubs and events, the colloquia and seminars, the paper discussions and guest lectures. Not to mention the research opportunities that'd be available after freshman year.

Then there were his fellow students, who were intelligent and interesting and tall and muscular and possessed the brightest smiles known to mankind and perfectly sculpted arms and... Okay, some of those might not be *all* the students. Or most of them, honestly. They might be statistical outliers and anomalies, in fact, but so what if his new friends didn't have those things? They *got* him. Their eyes didn't glaze over the moment he started talking about how much he was looking forward to solving differential equations.

And even better, he had people interested in *him*. People who thought he was funny and maybe a little attractive. People who invited him over for study sessions he'd assumed would be academically stimulating, only for him to find out his theoretical prediction had a mere fifty percent accuracy rate. Not that he was complaining when his lips were still tingling and his body was still buzzing from the less academic parts. Though he really should have been studying for finals.

He was smart enough to recognize that over the last few months, he'd begun to fill out and lose the gangliness of his high school growth spurt. Like his body had realized growing up wasn't just about getting taller. And while he wasn't, for example, a walking wet dream with... assets that had the kind of curvature that would make spacetime weep, he also wasn't entirely asset-less. Some people, at least, seemed to quite enjoy his assets. And it was important to carry out thorough experimentation, even if the absolute ideal test conditions were unavailable.

As Zayn opened the door to their room, the sight of Aiden sprawled out on his bed, reading their Intro to Astronomy textbook, greeted him.

Speaking of ideal test conditions. Zayn repressed a sigh.

Some celestial bodies were light-years out of reach, but that didn't make them less beautiful to observe.

Aiden glanced up, set his textbook aside, and grinned. Then he froze. He inhaled through his nose, his brow furrowing. His mouth opened and closed a few times before he asked, "How... how'd the study session go?"

Zayn's cheeks burned. "Um. Good. Really good."

"Oh. That's good."

For the first time in the months they'd lived together, the silence between them could have made space seem loud.

"So..." Aiden said, looking past Zayn. "I never asked. Are you, uh, seeing anyone?"

"Ah. Maybe? Sort of, I think?" They hadn't discussed labels, but they did have another study session planned for next week, and Zayn was fairly certain the amount of studying they'd be doing would be minimal.

Aiden stood abruptly. "Oh. That's cool. Yeah. Very cool. Right. I'm going to... Um. I think I forgot my copy of *Astronomy Essentials* in the library. Hopefully someone turned it in."

He slipped out the door before Zayn could point out that *Astronomy Essentials* was their Intro to Astronomy textbook. The one Aiden had been reading when he'd come in.

Zayn blinked at the door. What had just happened?

He picked up the textbook from Aiden's bed and set it on his desk, frowning.

Tomorrow was the full moon, and while every comprehensive study Zayn had ever read found no evidence of a link between lunar phases and human behavior, Aiden did seem to get twitchier in the days leading up to the opposition phase. And he was always gone the night of the full moon. Zayn hadn't noticed it at first, but a pattern appeared to be emerging.

He shook his head. No. He was imagining things. Anything else was sheer unscientific lunacy.

SEVEN

Aiden battled the urge to bounce his leg or get up and pace the room. He'd been jittery all day as he waited for the mage to arrive, and his nerves only got worse as evening neared. He'd never dealt with a mage before. One of their neighboring packs used to have a pack mage when he was a kid, but she'd died over a decade ago, and his alpha had never wanted him around the mage who ran the magic shop in town. The few times Aiden had passed by the shop as a teen had left his nose burning with the unpleasant reek of the mage's magic.

What would this mage do to Zayn? The lady on the phone had said they wouldn't hurt him. Zayn had done nothing wrong. MateHub had to realize that, right? If anything, they needed to track down the idiot who'd sent him the toy.

Aiden and Zayn were in their living room, doing home-work together, when the knock came.

"I'll get it." Aiden jumped to his feet and answered the door, then blinked at the man on the other side.

The guy was... smoking hot. Maybe in his late twenties

or early thirties. His jet-black hair fell loose and soft around his face, and the suit he was wearing fit him in a way that should have been illegal. Aiden's eyes slid down his body before he could stop them.

"If you're finished checking me out, I have business to take care of," the man said under his breath.

Aiden yanked his gaze back up, and his brain registered the scent of magic hanging off the man. The *mage*. The smell wasn't as unpleasant as Aiden had been prepared for, but it was still sharp and harsh.

"Sorry." Aiden cringed. He wasn't interested—he wasn't sure he *could* be interested in anyone other than Zayn—but he had eyes.

Zayn glanced up as Aiden let the mage in, his eyebrow quirking.

"This is..." Aiden trailed off. He didn't know the mage's name or how to introduce him. 'This is a mage, a thing you didn't realize was real, from MateHub, a site you can't access because you're unaware of the supernatural, here to talk to you about your new favorite toy, which you absolutely should not have. Oh, and I think he's about to put a spell on you,' didn't seem like the best explanation. But the mage stepped forward, offering his hand to Zayn.

"I'm Tristan Hasegawa, part of the project development team at M.H. Industries."

Zayn stood and shook his hand, looking confused. "M.H. Industries?"

"You might not have heard of us, but I believe you're familiar with one of our products."

A furrow formed between Zayn's brows. "M.H.? As in MateHub? I've been trying to find you online, but it's like you don't even exist."

Aiden couldn't breathe as he watched their conversation.

"About that," Tristan said. "There's been a bit of a mix-up on our part. You see, we've been developing a line of toys and had you listed as a potential reviewer for the finished products. Unfortunately, someone on our side got a little too excited and sent you a prototype before it was ready for market."

Zayn frowned. "You came here to tell me that? Where are you located? You couldn't have called or emailed?"

"Our headquarters are in LA, but I'm in the area on business, and we thought it'd be better if I stopped by in person to explain what happened."

"But... the package was sent anonymously to my PO box. Our apartment address isn't listed on my review site, just the PO. How did you know where I lived?"

Aiden's nose started to itch, the scent of magic suddenly sharper, the air in the room thick and heavy with it.

"Don't worry about that." Tristan's voice took on a smooth, mesmerizing quality. "I'm just here to ask you not to post your review until we're ready to launch."

Zayn opened his mouth to speak, then faltered. He tilted his head, confusion written in every line of his face. "Why..."

What the hell was this mage doing to Zayn? Aiden's wolf stirred, a low warning growl building in his throat. But the pressure of the magic was gone as quickly as it had increased, leaving behind only its abrasive scent.

"As I was saying, it's not quite ready for prime time, and we'd appreciate you holding off," Tristan said.

Zayn blinked, then focused on Tristan again, though bewilderment and confusion still hung around him like a swirling, dusty nebula. "The prototype seems pretty perfect to me."

"We're having a hard time ramping up production and don't want to launch until we can keep up with demand. Clearly this was our error, but if you're willing to wait, we're more than happy to make sure you're in the first wave of reviewers to get the final product. And we'll throw in a few of the other toys in the line as a bonus for the inconvenience."

"That's fair," Zayn said, seeming to shake off whatever Tristan had done to him. "I mean, I can't post a review of a product with no website or release date. But I'd like to keep the prototype, if possible."

Tristan smirked at him. "Enjoying it?"

"Best orgasm of my life. Whoever designed it gets my eternal love. I'm sad humans don't have that particular feature."

"If they did?"

"Oh, I'd be on that *so fast*."

Tristan chuckled and glanced at Aiden. "Well, I guess you'll have to settle for the prototype for now."

"Yeah, I've resigned myself to the fact that your toy has ruined human anatomy for me for life."

"I have a feeling you'll have other options shortly. I'll be in touch." Tristan turned and headed for the door, sending Aiden a look that was a clear 'follow me' as he did. He slipped outside and was gone.

Aiden stared at the door. "Ahhh. I... I'm going to see if he has a business card? Yeah. A card. In case you need to contact him."

He heard Zayn protest, but he followed Tristan out anyway.

Tristan wasn't difficult to find. The faint trail of magic led Aiden straight to him.

"Was that it?" Aiden asked as he walked up to him. "Was that the memory spell?"

"Oh, no. This was the initial assessment of his level of awareness and general demeanor. He seems clueless and amiable, so I'm not particularly concerned at the moment, but we'll have to get a memory spell in here and wipe his memory."

"But you did something to him? To his memory? Just now. I smelled it. What did you do?" Whatever it was, his wolf hadn't liked the idea of a mage messing with their... Zayn.

"He's a smart guy. Without a magical nudge, I doubt he would have stopped asking questions or believed that I drove six hours to an address I shouldn't know to request he not post a review. It's a temporary enchantment though. All it did was make him slightly less curious. He'll be full of questions again by tomorrow morning."

Well, that didn't make Aiden feel better. Zayn's curiosity was one of his defining traits; he always wanted to learn more, to experiment and question until he had the answers he needed. Aiden hated that someone could take that away from Zayn so effortlessly, even if the effect was temporary.

Tristan studied him coolly, and Aiden tried not to squirm under the scrutiny.

"You've been living together for over three years, right?"

"How do you know that?"

"We have our methods."

Well, that kind of freaked Aiden out. Between their "methods" and their tech mages' apparent abilities to censor the entire internet, he could only hope MateHub used its power for good.

"You are aware that memory spells are notoriously difficult to control, aren't you?" Tristan's tone was nonchalant. "We can't remove his memory of a single toy; we have to wipe it of all things supernatural."

Aiden's stomach lurched. "Does that mean... What about... Will he remember...?" He swallowed.

"It depends on whether or not his brain considers you supernatural. If he suspects something about you isn't human..." Tristan shrugged.

Aiden frowned. He'd always been careful around Zayn. He didn't think he suspected anything. Zayn was crazy smart, but in a scientific way. He wouldn't think werewolves and wizards were real, right?

"Of course, if he were to, let's say, learn about the supernatural and get bonded to a shifter, I wouldn't have to wipe his memory." Tristan's bored expression said he couldn't care less whichever way it went.

Aiden's frown deepened. "I don't know how my pack would react to me bonding a human, or how Zayn would react to finding out about the supernatural."

"Not my business. But generally speaking, not having to do a memory spell is much preferable. Human brains are annoyingly delicate to work with." He pulled out a card and handed it over. "Here's my number. Normally I'd do the spell within twenty-four hours, but I seem to have forgotten to bring salt."

"Salt?"

"For the spell."

"...Special salt?"

"Salt salt. You know. White stuff. Extremely difficult to come by or purchase. Very expensive. Foolish of me to forget it, really. Now I'll have to drive back to the MateHub headquarters to get some. At which point, I'm sure there will be a different fire for me to put out that'll take at least a week to handle."

Aiden breathed a little easier.

A week.

Okay.

That gave him time to decide what to do.

"And just so you know," Tristan said with flat disinterest. "MateHub is aware of Zayn's blog. He has quite a fanbase in the supernatural community. Obviously I can't make any offers, but if he knew about the supernatural, there'd be an audience for his reviews of our merchandise, provided they were hosted on a more appropriate, secure site. And if we were ever to make a more human-friendly line, it'd be useful to have a contact who reviews toys off-site as well, to help us drum up promo. Just saying."

With that, he nodded to Aiden, got into his car, and drove off.

Aiden stared after him for a long moment, then returned to the apartment.

"So..." Zayn said as Aiden entered. "He's... good-looking. A bit old, I guess. But good-looking."

Well, crap. Zayn thought he'd gone after Tristan for personal reasons.

"Uh, no," Aiden said. "He isn't my type." His type was very specific, and while Tristan was hot, he wasn't it.

Zayn almost looked relieved, though Aiden wasn't sure he wanted to let himself believe that.

He walked back to where they'd been studying and sat next to Zayn again, inhaling his perfect scent as he did.

Tonight, he would figure out what he was going to do

about Zayn, but first, they had a Cosmology assignment they needed to finish.

EIGHT

THEN

April, Freshman Year

Why would anyone in their right mind go to Cancun or Miami Beach or wherever for spring break when, just a few weeks later, they could do something like this? Camping in Joshua Tree National Park on a moonless night with clear skies, the Milky Way stretching out above them and the Lyrid meteor shower reaching its peak.

Zayn couldn't wait.

He and Aiden had set up their campsite earlier that day, and now they were lying outside their tent on their sleeping bags, settling in for the show.

Aiden was distractingly close. Zayn would barely need to move his arm for it to hit Aiden's, and that special brand of Aiden gravity—the one that had compelled Zayn to learn how to defy all laws of physics to resist its pull—was at its strongest when they were mere inches apart. Newton's law in textbook form; the strength of Aiden's gravitational force demanding Zayn's inevitable fall.

Not that he hadn't fallen months ago.

Aiden inhaled, taking an expansive breath that swelled his chest and bumped their arms together briefly, before he let it out in a shuddering sigh.

He did that sometimes, like he was never quite able to get enough air in his lungs. In Zayn's more delusional moments, he swore Aiden did it more often when they were close, maybe leaning in just to do it, but he had to be imagining that. There was no logical reason for Aiden to breathe Zayn in like he'd drown without him.

It didn't matter though; this was perfection.

"We should come out here during the next supermoon." Zayn would happily spend countless nights with Aiden under the stars.

Aiden froze for a second, then gasped. "*Oh.* I left my water bottle in the tent. I'm going to grab it. Need anything?"

Full moon. Right. Aiden wouldn't be around.

"I'm good. Here, I've got the—" Zayn cut himself off as Aiden got up and smoothly covered the few steps to their tent, then ducked inside. "...red light flashlight."

But Aiden didn't seem to be having any problem finding his water bottle without it.

"You must have excellent night vision," Zayn said as he returned.

"Ah, yeah. My eyes dark adapt quickly. It, uh, runs in my family."

When he lay down next to Zayn, he felt even closer than before.

A soft breeze rustled through the scattered desert

plants. Around them, a chorus of insects created a song of chirps and buzzes and clicks, punctuated by the occasional hoot of an owl and the yips of coyotes. Their melody drifted through peaks and valleys, slipping into caesuras of silent stillness so profound it was as if the Earth itself was holding its breath, and the only movement in the universe was the meteors falling above them.

"I wish we could bottle this and bring it back to the dorms," Zayn said in the softest of whispers, but Aiden heard him.

"The miracle that would have to happen to get things even a fraction as quiet as this."

Their neighbors on both sides seemed to hold grudges against the concept of silence, like it had killed their loved ones and they were on a mission to eradicate it out of existence. It made studying for tests a particular treat.

"What are you planning to do next year?" Aiden asked. "Dorms again?"

"I want to get an apartment off campus, but I'm not sure I can afford it."

Aiden hesitated before he said, "We could probably afford a place together. If you'd want that."

Their own place. Somewhere quiet where they'd be able to study without all the chaos of the dorms right outside their door. That would be amazing.

"I'd love that."

Zayn's cheeks hurt, he was grinning so hard, and when he glanced over, he felt the radiating brightness of Aiden's smile shining through the dark.

Yeah, they'd get a place together, and their sophomore year would be even better than their freshman one.

Aiden's hand brushed against his, but he didn't pull away. Neither did Zayn.

As they lay there in the tranquility of the desert night, under a sky full of infinite stars and possibilities, solitude and serenity a warm blanket wrapping around them and this moment, Zayn couldn't imagine ever wanting to be anywhere else in the entire universe.

NINE

NOW

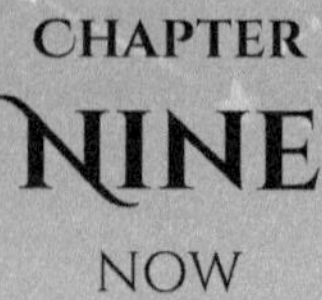

"What am I supposed to do?" Aiden groaned for the hundredth time that day.

"There's only one choice," Bram said. "You're going to have to give him the real version of that toy he loves so much. Absolutely Richard Knotz the hell out of him."

"Could you not joke about that?"

Bram chuckled. "Still jealous of a toy?"

Yes. Kind of. A lot. That didn't mean he had to respond to the comment. "But he's *human*."

"So what? Humans are tasty. I fully understand you wanting to sink your fangs in and drink him up."

Aiden ignored the idea of humans being tasty. "How can I tell him about the supernatural?"

"Dude, you aren't the first idiot to fall for a human. Talk to your alpha. There are probably protocols."

"We don't have any humans in our pack."

"I mean, I don't know shit about shifter politics, but if your alpha isn't willing to change that for your chosen mate, he isn't worthy of being an alpha."

"Hey. Grant's the best alpha."

"Then tell him you've been mooning over a human since freshman year and want him to be your mate."

"But what if it isn't that? What if it's some crush I've convinced myself is more than it is?"

"How does he smell to you?"

Aiden sighed. "Perfect."

"And how do you smell together?"

"Better than perfect."

"And how does your wolf feel about him?"

His wolf had been waiting for far too long for him to claim Zayn. To finally pull him into their arms, to do everything they'd ever fantasized about doing to him, to bite him, to make Zayn theirs. To give themselves to Zayn in return.

"From that spaced-out expression, it seems safe to assume your wolf approves."

Aiden shook himself and focused on Bram. "Completely."

"And when you imagine the two of you together, are you also imagining..." He made a fist and then slowly expanded his fingers.

Aiden swatted at his hand, but when that didn't stop Bram from looking like he was holding an invisible baseball, Aiden pushed him off the couch.

Bram laughed as he picked himself up and reclaimed his seat. "That wasn't a no."

It wasn't even close to a no. "Every single time."

"Yeah. Thought so. I don't need a shifter's sense of smell to recognize you're perfect for each other." He leaned back against the couch. "But how cool would it be if he did videos for MateHub? He'd get so many views."

Aiden suppressed a growl.

"You're trying not to growl, aren't you?"

Busted. Aiden huffed. He knew he was being unreasonable.

"*Solo* scenes. I'm not suggesting he let the real Richard rail him."

"I know," Aiden grumbled. "And I don't want him to stop filming his reviews, or for people to stop watching them. He enjoys them. Hell, I enjoy them. I just want people to realize they can only watch."

"You know one excellent way to do that, right?" Bram flashed his fangs and made a little biting motion.

"But seriously." Aiden sighed. "He'll never believe me."

"So shift in front of him."

"I don't want to freak him out. Like, 'hey, sit there while I strip—'"

"I'm pretty sure he'd be willing to do that part at least."

"And transform into a large wolf? He'd definitely freak out."

"Should I set you two up on another accidental date so you can make a move on him?"

"God, please no. The first dozen were more than enough, thanks."

"Fine. Be that way."

They sat there, thinking it over.

"Did you know that last year a human started doing scenes for MateHub?" Bram asked eventually. "Apparently his roommate showed him the site. You could do that. Say you want to show him the inspiration for that toy of his."

That was the worst idea Aiden had ever heard, but it wasn't like he'd come up with anything better.

Aiden tapped his foot against the floor as the video call connected.

"Aiden," Grant said when he answered, his chiseled features breaking into a warm smile. "What's up?"

"I kind of... fell in love with Zayn when we were freshmen and he smells amazing and I want to make him my mate but I need your permission because he's human and I'm not sure how to tell him so what do I do?"

Grant's laughter was soothing, a reminder of home and pack. "Well, first, I suggest breathing. That's usually a good start."

Aiden forced himself to take a deep breath. Huh, that did help. Grant might be onto something.

"Sorry. I didn't mean to, but he's so smart and awesome, and his scent is..." He sighed. "But he's also very human."

"And you're worried I'm going to be upset by that?"

"Maybe? I don't know. Our pack doesn't have any humans."

Grant's blue eyes glittered with mirth. "Yet. God, son, we've been wondering how long it'd take you to bring this up since the first time you came home smelling like him and then spent your entire break talking about him. I think Aiyana organized a betting pool your sophomore year."

Aiden blinked at the phone. "What?"

"You have my permission. I'll fill out the necessary paperwork for the council and submit it as soon as you're bonded. I'll send over a list of the information I need, but it's mainly date of birth and the like."

Well... that had been easier than he'd thought it would be. Too bad everything couldn't be that easy.

"But how should I tell him?"

"You know him best. But if it were me, I'd say I needed to talk to him about something important that might be difficult for him to believe. Explain it to him, then show him. It's pretty hard for people to deny the shift once they've seen it."

"What if he freaks out?"

"He likely will, at least a little."

"That's not comforting."

"He smells right?"

"He really does."

"Then trust your instincts. If you have feelings for him, the freaking out will be worth it."

Aiden exhaled. "Okay. I'll try."

Grant grinned. "Good. And bring him with you the next time you come home. We've been dying to meet him."

The idea of bringing Zayn home to meet his pack sent bubbly elation tingling through his body. "I will."

Now he just needed to figure out how to tell him.

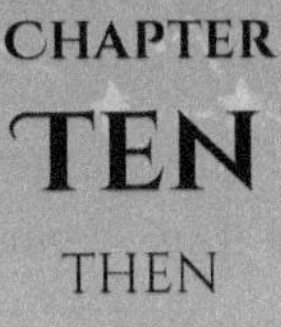

February, Sophomore Year

"How did you get these tickets again?" Zayn asked Aiden as they stood in a long line outside the university planetarium.

"Bram gave them to me. He said he'd planned to use them, but something came up, and he didn't want them to go to waste."

Zayn nodded. That made sense, and he'd always happily go to the planetarium, whatever they were showing for the night.

But when they got to the entrance, Zayn's eyebrows rose. A violently pink sign was stretched above the door, elaborate calligraphy declaring the event, *Written in the Stars: A One-of-a-Kind Valentine's Day Experience.*

He blinked at it, then pulled out his phone.

Oh. It was February fourteenth. He hadn't realized, but when he glanced around, he noticed the line consisted of nothing but obvious couples.

He looked up at Aiden, who was clearly having the same realization he was. So definitely no deeper, hidden meaning. Right. Not as if that thought had crossed Zayn's mind. After a year and a half of living together, he knew not to get his hopes up. But it was fine. It was the planetarium. He'd been there with Aiden dozens of times. This wouldn't be any different.

Except the smiling lady at the entrance had never handed him a large box of chocolates before.

"It's so great to see regulars here on a night like this," she said.

Aiden laughed nervously. "Yeah. Can't wait for the show."

They settled into their seats, their arms bumping against each other on the armrest between them as the lights dimmed and music swelled.

The show took them through a tour of constellations, each featuring a romantic tale written forever in the stars, from Perseus and Andromeda to Altair and Vega, even the lost Pleiad, Merope, and her love for the mortal Sisyphus.

It was terribly unscientific, but Zayn couldn't say he minded, not when Aiden was right there, his arm still brushing against Zayn's as they watched stars dance across the domed ceiling, the show reaching a climax with a dazzling display of shooting stars and swirling galaxies in the artificial sky above them.

No, he didn't mind at all.

ELEVEN

NOW

It was pouring, and there was no indication that would change anytime soon. While they could still head to the campsite they'd booked and hope things cleared up, Aiden recognized a lost cause when he saw one.

Zayn looked out of their apartment window and sighed before walking over to the couch and slumping down next to Aiden. When they were this close, it was impossible not to breathe him in, not to notice the heavenly combination of their scents on Zayn's skin.

"It should never be allowed to rain at night," Zayn said.

"I'd bet most people prefer it this way."

Zayn huffed. "Most people probably don't know there was a Kp8-level coronal mass ejection yesterday, and between that and the new moon, tonight should have been optimal viewing for aurorae."

"They probably don't." Aiden bit back a grin. It would have been amazing to do their usual routine of staying up all night, basking in the glow of the stars. Though that was more Zayn's routine. Aiden often got distracted by other beautiful sights.

But maybe this was a sign. He'd been trying to find the courage to talk to Zayn, and now they had nothing to do for the night. It was time to get his shit together and tell Zayn. Though, after multiple days of brainstorming, he still only had one idea of how to approach the subject, as ridiculous as it was.

If this went poorly, he was blaming Bram. But he knew Zayn was observationally oriented. He'd never believe Aiden if he were to casually say, "Hey, so, funny story. I'm a werewolf." He'd need proof.

Aiden let out an unsteady exhale, and Zayn raised an eyebrow at him.

"So…" Nervous sweat prickled on Aiden's neck. "You know that toy you got sent?"

"I am quite familiar with Mr. Knotz, yes."

Aiden was not going to growl over a toy. He exhaled again. "I, uh, found something related you might like."

Zayn's eyebrows rose even higher.

God, this was the worst idea ever. Aiden took out his laptop and navigated through his bookmarks to the links he'd saved in case he ended up doing this extremely ill-advised thing.

"You have a miscellaneous folder inside a miscellaneous folder inside a different miscellaneous folder? Are you about to show me porn?"

"Um." Well, what had he expected? Zayn was a genius, after all.

"Was a taxes folder not obvious enough for—" Zayn cut himself off as the site loaded. He sat up straighter, his gaze flickering to Aiden before returning to the screen. "Mate-Hub? Their site is online? I keep checking, but nothing comes up."

"Yeah, there's a reason for that. It's… paywalled, among

other protections. I'll explain in a minute. But first, here's their merch shop."

He held out the laptop, and Zayn's eyes widened to an extent that would have been comical if Aiden weren't five seconds away from a panic attack.

"Mr. Knotz! Number one bestseller. I knew it. But what is this? 'See the whole Shifter Line'?" He reached over and clicked the banner. "Wolf and canine shifters, feline shifters, bear shifters. What are shifters? Do they all change somehow? Like the knot? Is that shifting? Oh. Hello, Mr. Shark Shifter. Wait. These are on sale already? Can I order them? My viewers are going to love these."

Aiden couldn't keep his nerves out of his voice as he answered. "Right. That's the thing. Most of your viewers can't... love them."

"Why not?" Zayn shot him a confused look.

"Let me show you the inspiration for Mr. Knotz."

"I mean, I'm not a zoology major, but I can guess, and I'm not interested in seeing that."

"I think you will be." Aiden's chuckle sounded strained to his own ears, but he clicked on the video he'd book-marked. It was easy to find the time stamp he was looking for—the most watched part.

"*Oh.* You really are showing me porn," Zayn said, a hint of breathiness to his words.

Aiden was fairly certain his lungs had stopped working as he hit play. Lewd moans and the slick slap of skin against skin filled the room.

Zayn glanced at him again, then back to the screen where the camera was zooming in for a nice close-up as Richard Knotz started to demonstrate why he was a legend, his knot swelling, his thrusts becoming more forceful to fuck it in and out of his co-star. Aiden saw the exact moment Zayn registered what was happening.

"Wha—?" Zayn cut himself off, his mouth falling open, his brow furrowing. He narrowed his eyes at the screen and leaned in. "Is that…? How are they…? Wait. Is that a cock sleeve? Do they sell that? Can I get one?" He tilted his head. "But it's so seamless. That can't be it. Is it CGI? No. There's no way. It's too realistic." His gaze stayed trained on the video, like if he stared hard enough, it'd make sense to him.

On screen, Richard thrust in a final time, his knot fully expanding, locking him inside his co-star. He started to grind instead, his co-star shaking, nearly sobbing with ecstasy as he writhed, his hands tugging on Richard, trying to pull him closer, but Richard kept enough space between them to ensure the cameras could get the shots they needed.

Zayn wet his lips, then swallowed audibly.

Fuck, he smelled turned on. It took all of Aiden's willpower not to lean in and drown himself in Zayn's scent on an average day, but like this, Zayn stirred instincts in him he couldn't deny.

Usually on new moons, his wolf was at its quietest, but not tonight, not with Zayn smelling like that over the idea of being knotted. His wolf rumbled, the sound resounding in Aiden's chest. Zayn's head whipped toward him.

Aiden felt his wolf surge forward, just below the surface, wanting everything Aiden's strange human sensibilities had denied them for years.

Zayn flinched. "Your eyes. They flashed…" His breathing accelerated as his gaze jumped between Aiden and the laptop, a high-pitched note of something in his tone—not panic, but close. "Aiden, what's a shifter?"

Pausing the video, Aiden set the laptop aside. "The top?

His name is Richard Knotz. He's a wolf shifter. It means he can..." He took a deep breath, then rushed forward. "He can transform into a wolf."

"Like... a werewolf?"

"Kind of. Except we have control over it."

"*We?*"

"Yeah. We." Aiden tried to smile reassuringly, but he didn't need a mirror to know it was a painfully awkward expression.

Zayn sat, blinking rapidly. "You. You can transform into a wolf?"

"I can show you, but please don't freak out?"

Zayn nodded numbly, and Aiden stood, stripping off his shirt, then unbuttoning his jeans.

"What... what are you... why?" Zayn asked, his eyes latching onto Aiden's hands as they eased down his zipper.

"Clothes don't shift with us."

"Oh. Oh, yeah. Of course. That's... logical?" He didn't look away when Aiden pushed down his jeans.

Aiden had never been shy about being naked—very few shifters were—but having Zayn watch him strip made him feel clumsy as he stepped out of his boxer briefs. Though with Zayn's attention on him, on his body, he also wanted to stay in this form, standing there until Zayn had looked his fill.

But he had to do this.

"Zayn," he said gently, and Zayn's eyes darted up to meet his. "Before I shift, I need you to know I would never hurt you. Whatever form I'm in, you're safe."

"I know." Zayn sounded like he meant it. Whether or not he'd still feel that way when Aiden was a wolf remained to be seen.

Aiden gave himself over to the shift, letting the pleasure

and pain of it ripple through his body, keeping his gaze locked on Zayn as much as he could during the transformation.

To his credit, Zayn didn't completely freak out, though he did pull back when Aiden took a cautious step toward him.

Zayn inhaled sharply. "You're insanely strong. You see better in the dark than any human should. You're always gone on the full moon."

Aiden dipped his head in acknowledgment, taking another step forward when Zayn reached out a shaky hand.

Zayn's laughter was equally unsteady. "I thought I was going crazy over the last few years because I'd have these moments when I'd think I was imagining the things I've seen you do. My brain kept trying to tell me something about you didn't add up, but I figured that was insane. It wasn't logical." He brushed tentative fingers against Aiden's fur.

Aiden forced himself to stay still, to not lean into that touch, no matter how tempting it was.

"Why didn't you tell me?"

He couldn't answer that in this form, so he shifted back to human, now kneeling in front of Zayn.

"Does that hurt?"

"A little. But it also feels amazing." He paused, looking up at Zayn, then answered his other question. "I'm sorry. We rarely tell humans. Keeping this secret is drilled into us from birth. It has to be secret for us to be safe."

Zayn gave a slow nod. "So why are you telling me now?"

"That toy? It never should have been sent to you. The reason you couldn't find the MateHub website is because only people who are aware of the supernatural can access it. It's protected by magic so humans can't find it."

"Magic? Does that mean there are... wizards? Witches?"

"Mages, but yes."

"*Mages.*" He sat for a minute, eyes unfocused as he tried to process that. "Wait. Bram? Is he a shifter too? Or a mage?"

"No. He's..." Aiden laughed nervously. "He's a vampire."

"A *vampire.* Vampires are real?"

"Yes. And some others too, like incubi and fae."

"Oh. I suppose, with a name like Bram, I should have guessed."

Aiden snorted. "His full name is Abraham, but his parents are absolute menaces. They named their kids after famous authors of vampire fiction. Abraham, Sheridan, Anne, Stephen. When Bram complained about their names, they told him he should be glad they didn't go with their first choices, which were Vlad, Lestat, Carmilla, and Orlok."

"They're *all* vampires?"

"Yeah. Generally speaking, being a vampire is a family thing, like being a shifter."

"Right. Of course." Zayn sounded a bit faint.

"You're freaking out, aren't you?"

"Just... just a little. I mean, it's not every day you find life outside the world you live in. I've always wanted to discover extraterrestrial life. Discovering *extra* terrestrial life hadn't even crossed my mind."

Aiden couldn't help but grin. Leave it to Zayn to make an exoplanet joke while he was shell-shocked.

"Could you..." Zayn's gaze traveled down Aiden's body, then jerked back up. "I can't believe I'm about to ask this, but could you put your clothes on, please?"

Oh, oops. He was still naked. "Sorry."

Zayn shook his head, but he did seem to focus better

after Aiden was dressed and sitting on the couch with him again.

"Okay. So, the toy. One of my viewers sent it, which means they're a shifter or something?"

"We think so."

"Will they get in trouble?"

"If they're found? Probably. It was reckless of them to send it to you."

"But it's okay for you to tell me?"

"In this particular case, yes. I've gotten permission. But I need you to promise not to tell anyone."

"Absolutely. I understand why you have to keep it secret, and I don't want anything to happen to you."

Aiden hadn't honestly believed Zayn would expose them, but it was a relief to hear him say it.

"This is why you're never around on the full moon?"

"Yeah. On full moons, we tend to look less human. It's harder to hide, harder to control our instincts. It's too far to go home every month, but there's a local pack I'm, like, a temporary member of. I run with them on those nights. It helps soothe my wolf's need to be around pack."

Zayn's eyes caught on the laptop. "And... knotting?"

"Yeah. For wolf and other canine shifters."

"So you have...?"

"Not exactly. Not yet, at least."

"Not yet?"

Aiden forced out an exhale. Okay. Here it was. The most nerve-racking part. "We only have knots after we bond a mate." He already saw the questions forming in Zayn's mind, so he continued. "Bonding is sort of the shifter version of marriage. The shifter bites their mate, and a connection forms between them, an emotional link that lets you feel your mate, and lets them feel you in return. It's supposed to be intense."

Zayn frowned at the laptop. "That was Richard Knotz and his mate?"

"Ah. That's complicated. Richard Knotz is a special case. He bonds co-stars for his scenes so he can knot them. Most shifters could never do what he does. Normally, you bond after you find a compatible mate."

"Compatible? As in, you get along well? But it doesn't seem like you're using the human meaning of the word."

"I'm not. It's similar, but for us, there's more to it. It's in our scents. Every shifter, every mage, every human, we all have unique scents. When two people are truly compatible, their scents combine in a way that's more than the sum of their parts. Both complete on their own, but infinitely better together."

"Binary stars that balance each other with their gravitational pull?"

Aiden nodded and steeled himself. "We don't tell humans this. If a human finds out, a mage makes them forget about it."

"That guy from MateHub? Tristan?"

"Yeah."

"He's going to make me forget this?" Zayn's expression was upset enough that it made Aiden hurry on.

"The only humans who are ever told, the only time permission is ever given to tell a human, is when a shifter is compatible with them. When the shifter thinks they could be their mate." He swallowed the lump in his throat and watched the realization dawn on Zayn's face.

"Me? You think I could be your... mate?"

"Not *think*. I *know* you could be. If you wanted to be."

"We smell good together?"

"You're all honey and an early fall breeze rustling through leaves, and I'm sort of warm spices and the harvest moon, and together, we combine into a scent better than anything I've ever smelled before."

Zayn stared at him, more than a little stunned.

"It's a lot, and you don't have to decide now—"

But Zayn was shaking his head. "No. I mean, yeah, it's a lot. I have so many questions, and I'm not sure I understand this whole bonding thing, but I want to be with you. I've been trying not to fall in love with you since you talked about exoplanets on move-in day, and I think I gave up even trying sometime during our sophomore year. Maybe I can't tell what we smell like, but I don't need to. I know we'd be perfect together. So bite me, bond me, knot me, whatever you want to do to me. I'm yours."

Relief washed over Aiden, but there was one more thing he needed confirmation on. "I know the answer is no, and I hate that I'm asking this, but it's not because I have... Well, you really like that toy."

Zayn shook his head again. "We could spend the rest of our lives with me topping you, or us never doing that at all, and I would be okay with it. I mean, I do prefer to bottom, and I'd be using the hell out of Mr. Knotz, but I don't care as long as I'm with you. Whatever that entails. Knot or, well... not."

Aiden felt himself grinning. "Same. I've wanted to be with you forever, but I wasn't sure how to tell you about this. I was worried it'd freak you out. That I might lose you as a friend. And I'd rather love you from afar and pine after you for the rest of my life than do that."

"We're idiots, aren't we?"

No one in their right mind would call Zayn that. Aiden,

on the other hand, was fully deserving of that label, but he was going to fix that.

He brushed his fingers along Zayn's cheek, grazing skin he'd longed to touch for years. "Can I kiss you?"

A smile played at the corner of Zayn's mouth, desire kindling in his eyes, and he nodded, sending a jolt of anticipation through Aiden.

Aiden's fingers stilled, his hand shaking slightly as he hesitated, but then Zayn was leaning in, and Aiden forgot how to breathe. His heart pounded as Zayn's lips hovered close to his. He'd lost count of the fantasies he'd had about doing this.

"I've always thought," Zayn said, the words a whisper of breath against Aiden's skin, "that you have this special kind of gravity. It's so much stronger than any formula or theorem could ever account for. The way I'm drawn to you... it's inescapable, inevitable."

That resonated deep in Aiden's soul. "I thought us being together was impossible, but after all the time I've spent staring up at the night sky, I should have known. With all the planets and galaxies in the universe, with all the infinite number of iterations that exist, the impossible can happen when the right stars align." He closed the last fraction of distance between them, his eyelids fluttering shut as their lips met.

It was sweet and gentle, an exploration, a promise fulfilled, but that delicate touch left Aiden breathless, electricity sparking through his veins as Zayn moved in closer, settling into his lap. He let Zayn have control, let him tip his head back and deepen the kiss. If he'd thought Zayn smelled good, it was nothing compared to how he felt, how he tasted.

He could search the cosmos until the stars went dark,

but he'd never find something as extraordinary as this, as them together.

A pleased rumble built in Aiden's chest, his hands gripping Zayn's hips tighter, and Zayn gasped into his mouth, breaking apart to ask, "What do you like?"

Aiden froze, causing Zayn to pull away farther—the opposite of what he wanted.

"I... don't know?" Aiden said, answering the question in Zayn's gaze.

Zayn frowned. "You don't know what you like?"

"Ah." Aiden was back to chuckling awkwardly. "I've never done more than this." And even *this* he hadn't done often.

"But you're... Have you seen yourself? Don't people throw themselves at you?"

Aiden shrugged. "In high school I messed around with a friend a few times. And I did try during our freshman year, but it was never what I actually wanted. It never felt right, especially when I couldn't stop thinking about you, no matter who I was with."

"Oh. Sorry. I didn't know. I mean, obviously. If I'd known..."

Aiden shook his head. "Seeing you with other people, smelling them on you, hurt. But it's not a bad thing one of us knows what the hell we're doing."

As much as each new boyfriend had stung, Aiden had loved watching Zayn find himself, growing from the timid boy who had walked into their dorm room to the gorgeous, confident person he was now.

"Well," Zayn said, smiling. "In that case, some thorough experimentation is in order."

Aiden returned the grin. Yes. Yes, it was.

Zayn slid off his lap and lay back on the couch, his hand

twisted in Aiden's shirt. "Okay, first experiment. Let's start where most people likely start. The wonderful force that is friction."

Aiden let himself be pulled down onto Zayn, settling between his legs, the thrill of it singing in his blood. He'd already been hard from their kisses, but this, having Zayn under him, pressed against him, was the most turned on he'd ever been.

He braced himself on his forearms, but that wasn't close enough for either of them. Zayn wrapped his arms and legs around Aiden, tugging him closer until their whole bodies were flush against each other.

Their lips met again, and Aiden's thoughts scattered like light hitting Earth's atmosphere—dazzling and fragmented and incandescent from all the sensations rushing through him.

"Do whatever feels good." Zayn's grip tightened on his shoulders.

Aiden leaned down, nuzzling into Zayn's neck, lost in the scent of him, the honeyed arousal that made his canines ache to drop, to bite, to claim. Zayn shivered, a tiny gasp escaping him as Aiden's blunt teeth grazed his skin.

How many times had he imagined Zayn making sounds like that for him?

He rocked against Zayn, their hard lengths pressing together, far too many layers of clothes between them, but still so, so good. The friction set him ablaze with heat, alight with a fire of want and need so bright and scorching it threatened to consume every molecule of his being.

No two bodies, celestial or otherwise, fit together as perfectly as this. Zayn clung to him, moving with him, letting out breathy moans with each roll of Aiden's hips.

Aiden groaned, the sensation almost too intense. He

wanted Zayn's skin against his, but he couldn't pull away to make that happen. Rutting against Zayn filled him with a heady pleasure, the grind of their hips too intoxicating to stop.

"You feel so good." Zayn's voice trembled as he panted against Aiden's ear. "I can't wait to feel you in me, bonding me, knotting me."

Aiden rocked into him harder, his pace building to an urgent rhythm that matched the pounding of his heart, the rushing of blood in his ears.

The universe collapsed under the immense gravity between them, pressure coiling deep in Aiden until he was strung so tight there was nothing left but for him to explode. He cried out, his hips jerking as he fell apart, as shock waves of energy pulsed through him. As Zayn's scent and taste and touch made him feel like they could outshine entire galaxies when they were together.

He sank down next to Zayn, his breathing rough. Even though they hadn't bonded yet, it felt like the fundamental elements of his being were rearranging themselves, like some part of him was giving itself to Zayn until they were an inseparable whole.

Aiden smiled into the crook of Zayn's neck, inhaling him like oxygen until Zayn shifted, turning his head to look at him. Aiden brushed his thumb over his lips, then pulled him in for a kiss. It was equal parts sweet and gentle, passionate and intense, full of affection and desire.

Zayn's hips flexed against his thigh, the insistent press of his dick unmistakable. Aiden glanced down, then back at Zayn. "Can I...?"

"Yes. Anything you want, yes."

Aiden palmed him through his jeans, watching Zayn's

eyes slide shut as he bit his lip, though that didn't stop his groan.

Taking someone else out of their pants was both awkward and thrilling, but the hot weight of Zayn in his hand felt right in ways he'd never be able to properly describe.

Aiden hesitated for a moment, then ran his fingers over Zayn's shaft, feeling the silky skin and the hardness beneath. His first few pulls were tentative, but Zayn bucked into the touch, his breath hitching, and Aiden realized he knew this. He knew Zayn's body, knew what he liked, the rhythm he used when he was about to come. It wasn't difficult for him to match, not when every stroke was earning him desperate moans, Zayn clinging to him as he got closer and closer to the edge. He writhed against Aiden, his cries choking off as he came, splattering Aiden's hand with his release, and Aiden worked him through it until Zayn was softening in his grip.

They lay there in the afterglow, the blissed-out expression on Zayn's face more than Aiden could have ever asked for, the knowledge that he'd done that to Zayn, that he'd made him come, impossibly sweet. His wolf was a contented warmth in his chest. It still wanted more, but it was satisfied for now.

"God," Zayn said, his voice rough, "that was exactly how I jerk myself off."

"Ah, I know," Aiden admitted, letting out a nervous gust of laughter.

Zayn peeled his eyes open and looked at him.

"I, uh, have a membership to your site. And have watched your reviews. Every single one. I've probably gotten off to them more than I have to MateHub."

The smile Zayn gave him was brighter than anything Aiden had ever seen.

"Really? Because I think about you pretty much every time I film, maybe with the exception of the weird tentacle toys. For those, I'm mainly thinking, 'Why did someone make this?'"

He'd never seemed to be a fan of those.

"So, findings of the initial experiment? Objectives achieved and positive, replicable results yielded?" Zayn asked.

Aiden snorted. "I'd call it a resounding success. Hypothesis thoroughly supported and outcomes significantly better than predicted."

"Thoughts on what additional experiments you'd like to carry out?"

"Is 'all of them' an option?"

"Absolutely. And I have some toys you can try too, if you want." Aiden's eyes went wide, but Zayn continued quickly. "*Beginner* toys. We can go from there if you like them. I'm not expecting you to ride Mr. Knotz right out of the gate."

Oh, thank god.

"Though," Zayn said, "I'm just going to float this. If you do end up liking it, the idea of you with a toy knotted inside you while you knot me? Ridiculously hot."

Aiden shivered at the thought. It wasn't even remotely unappealing. "I'm not saying no, but when we're bonded, we'll each sense what the other is experiencing. So if I knot you, I'll feel what you're feeling, with or without the toy."

"And I'll feel it from your side too?"

"Yeah."

Zayn's eyes darkened. "We should do that."

Aiden couldn't have agreed more. Maybe a few experiments before then, but they definitely should.

He shifted his weight on the couch, then grimaced, the cooling mess in his pants reminding him of the results of their experiment.

"Cleanup time?" Zayn asked.

"Yes, and maybe future experiments could involve less of me coming in my underwear?"

"That, we can do," Zayn said, his words filled with promise. "I can suggest a place or two I'd rather have you come in next time." He ran a finger across his bottom lip.

Aiden let out a shuddering breath, unable to look away from his mouth. If Zayn kept doing things like that, next time wouldn't be too far off.

They hauled each other up from the couch and headed to the bathroom. Cleaning up involved more making out than Aiden would have imagined, and when they were finished, Zayn led him to his room, to his bed.

The heavy rain outside pounded against the roof, the steady sound lulling them to sleep. As Aiden drifted off with Zayn tucked against his chest, all he could think was that if every overcast night were like this, he wouldn't care if he never got to see the stars again.

TWELVE

THEN

May, Sophomore Year

The problem with having a regular sex life and then going into a sex slump was that Zayn still wanted to get off, and as great as his hand and fingers could be, he was finding himself... constrained by instrumental limitations.

He eyed the discreet brown box he'd set on his bed after it'd been delivered a few hours earlier, then turned back to his Galactic Astronomy textbook. Finals were in a few weeks, and he needed to finish this assignment so he could study for them.

Tapping his pencil against his desk, he forced himself to read the chapter on collisions and mergers, but no matter how many times he reread it, his brain refused to process the words on the page. He kept getting distracted by a section about galaxies colliding after multiple close encounters, their trajectories and gravitational interactions altering, drawing them closer and closer.

He swallowed and glanced over at the box. Had it

gotten bigger? It certainly seemed to be taking up more space in the room than before.

No, he was imagining things. Boxes didn't get bigger.

And he hadn't given up on dating, exactly; he'd simply had his whole college sexual awakening already. He'd done his experimenting, tried most of what he'd wanted to try, and now knew what he liked and didn't.

It'd been fun. Enjoyable. But nothing more than that. He'd had a whole series of sort-of boyfriends. None had been what he was looking for, but that was okay. A lot of people didn't date. Aiden had never mentioned anything about a boyfriend. Though, given how gorgeous he was, he'd easily get anyone he wanted. He probably hooked up regularly and just didn't tell Zayn the details.

Was that what he always did on full moons? Some weird moonlit orgy? It was about as plausible as Zayn's other theories to explain Aiden's repeated absences.

Zayn shook his head and tried to concentrate. Homework. He had homework to do.

Galactic collisions occurred slowly, two or more galaxies first brushing up against each other, gravitational forces pulling them together, causing their particles to mingle and unite. And then, depending on their sizes, on their angles and velocities, it might end with a complete and total merger, bursts of stars forming as they succumbed to those intense tidal interactions.

He sighed. Maybe he wasn't feeling Galactic Astronomy at the moment. That was fine. He had other subjects to study.

The box taunted him from his bed as he grabbed his Stellar Astrophysics textbook and flipped it open to the reading assignment. He didn't need to think about the box or Aiden or anything other than his homework.

This week they were covering chapter eight, which was on... pulsating stars and their rhythmic expansions and contractions, how hot and big they were, how they pulsed at different rates. A star might contract under the tight clench of gravity, becoming hotter and brighter until the nuclear reaction in its core created enough energy to expand it, swelling it larger, filling the empty, aching space around it, only to be clenched tight by gravity again.

He dropped his head to the desk and groaned. Why couldn't he focus? Why was his brain fixating on the largest box in the known universe looming in his peripheral vision?

Fine. There was no helping it. He'd take care of the reason he couldn't study, then finish his homework. That was clearly the most logical thing to do in this situation.

He peeked at the box. Yeah. Logical. That was what he'd do.

Aiden was out for the day. Why not test his hypothesis that he'd study better after a short break? In fact, he was certain he'd find sufficient evidence to support his claims.

He stood and picked up the box, but when he opened it, he frowned at the toy inside. The product information had claimed it was a 'Highly realistic experience! Lifelike quality!' This was not that. Not even close.

Since when had any erection been all one color? And particularly this color? Like someone had melted a bunch of peach crayons and remolded them into a penis and testicles. If a person's lower anatomy looked like this in real life, he might suggest they see a urologist. It could not be healthy.

He pulled out the product box, his brow furrowing when he removed the dildo and found it to be far from the promised 'true-to-life' silicone feel. While it wasn't hard plastic, it also wasn't fooling anyone.

Oh well. He'd bought it, he might as well give it a try.

Even though Aiden wasn't home, Zayn felt the need to sneak to the bathroom to give the toy and himself a thorough wash, like Aiden would pop out of nowhere and ask him what he was hiding under his shirt.

When he got back to his room, he shut the door and stripped. Air whispered over his skin, and he shivered.

It was time to see if this thing performed better than it looked.

As he settled onto his bed, nervous excitement fluttered in his chest. He'd experimented with his sort-of boyfriends, but he'd never used a toy before—an oversight on his part. With Aiden gone, he had plenty of time to explore this new acquisition without interruptions.

Taking a deep breath, he pulled the lube out of his nightstand, slicked up his fingers, and brought them to his hole, teasing his entrance. He trailed over the sensitive skin with a light touch.

Aiden had the prettiest hands. His fingers were long and thick, but he was so careful when he was handling delicate equipment. Zayn bit his lip as he sank two fingers into his ass. They weren't nearly thick enough for what he wanted, but he pushed them in and out while he jerked himself off with his other hand.

He kept his preparations to a minimum, then spread lube on the toy and lined it up, its silicone tip nudging against him.

With a deliberate, careful motion, he pushed the cool toy against his entrance, feeling it breach his rim. The initial stretch faded as he adjusted to the intrusion.

It felt disconnected and impersonal. Obviously. Every time he'd been in this position before, he'd had a warm body on top of him, and this was a sad replacement for the throbbing heat of another person pressing into him. Looking down and seeing the unnatural peachy length disappearing inside him didn't help matters.

He closed his eyes and pumped the toy in and out, trying to enjoy the unfamiliar sensation. There were benefits; he could admit that much. It penetrated deeper than his fingers, and its rigidity offered a novel stimulation to his prostate. The girth was decent—enough for a pleasant stretch, but not so much it was trying to bisect him.

How thick was Aiden? He had to be thicker than this. Likely longer too. The most worn of his sweatpants hinted at that much.

Anytime they were near each other, warmth all but radiated off Aiden. How would it feel to have Aiden on him, in him, stretching him open?

A moan slipped past Zayn's lips, visceral images flashing behind his eyes. Aiden thrusting into him, his strong arms enveloping him, holding him close. Their panting breaths mingling as they gasped into each other's mouths, Aiden's heat sinking into him, their sweat-slick bodies moving together in a cosmic dance.

Zayn wrapped a hand around himself and stroked in time to the fantasy. Aiden moving in him, grinding into him, taking him in an unyielding rhythm, bringing him to the edge. As the scene played in his mind, he quickened his pace, his strokes becoming more purposeful.

He clenched on the toy as he came, barely choking back a cry of Aiden's name, his hips jerking, pleasure coursing through him.

Then he collapsed onto the bed, panting and staring up at the ceiling. The hard silicone was unpleasant in his ass, so he slid it out.

Well, that had been a decent orgasm—better than the

majority he'd had with most of his sort-of boyfriends—but it hadn't been thanks to this thing.

On the plus side, he didn't feel as guilty over fantasizing about Aiden while using the toy. Sure, he still felt bad, but it wasn't compounded by the fact that he was doing it while he was with someone else. He'd have to find a toy he enjoyed at least as much as his fantasies, though that might be a tall order.

Grabbing a tissue, he wiped himself down before pulling on his clothes. He should clean himself and the toy up again.

He opened his bedroom door, then immediately slammed it shut.

Oh, crap. When had Aiden gotten home?

He cracked his door open, peering down the hall into the living room. Yep. That was Aiden sitting on their couch, a pillow in his lap as he scrolled on his phone.

"Hey," Zayn said, his voice high-pitched and strangled. "How long have you been home?"

"Uh. Um. Now? Like, a minute ago. Max." Aiden was looking everywhere but Zayn. "Definitely not any longer than that."

"Oh. That's cool. Totally cool. Thanks!" Zayn retreated into his room.

Okay then. He'd clean up later. After Aiden was asleep. Yeah. That was the best plan.

He winced.

Note for future experiments: make absolutely, *absolutely* sure Aiden was not coming home anytime soon.

But for now, he was going to distract himself from what had just happened.

As he eyed the dildo, with its bizarre peachy color and disappointing lack of realism, an idea hit him. He knew what he could do. He pulled up the product page and stared at it.

How did one rate a sex toy? There were several factors that should be included. Cost, feel, appearance, usability, packaging, quality of materials, experience of use... He outlined the necessary elements for a thorough review. Of course he'd start with a clear and concise title. That was easy.

The Disappointment of Over-promised Realism:
Insights and Observations

Then he needed a good abstract with an overview of his key findings, an introduction to the product itself, perhaps with some supplementary materials—photographs of the packaging and toy to show its true appearance as opposed to the manufacturer's promotional images. That should be followed by his methods of testing, the results, a thorough discussion of the relevant factors, and a solid conclusion.

Yeah, that sounded like a proper review. It wouldn't take long, and people should be informed before they spent money on an inferior toy.

He nodded to himself and got to work, his fingers flying over the keyboard until he hit the last paragraph.

Conclusion
While this toy provided some measure of assistance, allowing me to achieve orgasm, it was an overall lack-luster experience. Two stars. And not even a good two stars. We aren't talking about the Albireo binary system here. It's much more Struve 2398 level. You'll have to put in more work to find your target object than can truly be justifiable at this price.

He skimmed through what he'd written and nodded again. This was precisely the kind of review he would have wanted to see before purchasing this toy. Hopefully it would help future customers avoid making the same mistake he'd made.

But when he went to copy it into the review box, it got cut off by the character limit. Only a quarter of his review fit, the formatting was all wrong, and he couldn't upload his supplementary materials.

Fine. He'd host the review elsewhere and post his abstract to the product page with a link to the full text for those who wished to know more about his methodology and conclusions. That wouldn't be difficult to do.

A half hour later, he was the brand-new owner of his very own blog. InZayn Reviews: For Reviews of Everything In Zayn.

Perfect.

He let out a satisfied sigh and closed the browser. An afternoon well spent educating people.

Then his eyes landed on his textbooks. Oh crap. That was right. He had homework he was supposed to be doing and finals to study for.

At least now he'd be able to focus.

In the morning, he was surprised to find four comment notifications and that half a dozen people had subscribed to his blog. He hadn't realized they could do that, but apparently, they'd be getting emails whenever he posted something, and the comments were encouraging.

Anonymous:
Ripping shit apart scientifically. NICE. Can't wait for the next one. I'm going to share this with my friends.

Anonymous:
i need more of this in my life. please tell me you'll be doing more reviews?

Anonymous:
WHAT'S STRUVE 2398????

Anonymous:
Next time, include pictures of your 'methodology' with your supplementary materials.

Zayn frowned. He didn't know how he felt about that. Anyone could view this blog. It didn't seem like a good idea to post pictures like *that* publicly. If he were to post that sort of thing, he'd want a way to limit access to make sure everyone was of legal age at the very least. Hmm. For now, he'd stick to this format, though he might consider it in the future.

But first, he should order a few more toys and see how it went.

THIRTEEN

NOW

Dating Zayn somehow changed everything and almost nothing in Aiden's life. They still hung out together, still studied together, still did the things they'd done before, but now with stolen kisses, little touches, and the promise of coming home to do more than that. It was their friendship, yet so much better, so much more.

They'd tried to brainstorm date ideas they'd always hoped to do with someone special, but had found they'd already done them all, with the exception of one.

"Now that I know what you are, can we do a moon viewing?" Zayn had asked, and Aiden couldn't refuse a request like that. He'd wanted to spend a full moon with Zayn for years.

They even managed to snag a cabin tucked along the edge of Joshua Tree for the occasion, isolated so there were no other houses or people in sight. Just them and the moon and stars. Some light pollution stained the horizon, but not enough to dim the beauty of the night.

A gentle breeze blew over the landscape, carrying the faint aroma of desert plants and parched earth, though Zayn's scent was better than anything nature had to offer.

As the moon rose, so bright and full even Zayn had no trouble seeing, they sat on the cabin's porch and bathed in the moonlight. The night lay serene around them, the weather ideal, not a cloud in the sky.

It should have been perfect, but Aiden couldn't sit still. The call of the moon sang in his blood. The needs of his wolf simmered right under the surface, barely contained. He itched to run, to give in to his instincts, to claim Zayn as his own, but he also wanted to savor this experience.

Zayn glanced over at him, and when Aiden looked back, he knew his eyes flashed with his wolf.

"You're different tonight. Wilder, somehow. This is what you meant when you said you were less human on a full moon?"

Aiden nodded. "Our energy is tied to the moon. On full moons, that energy is at its peak. That's part of why we shift and run. It helps use some of that excess."

"Do you need to do that?"

Aiden shook his head. He had no desire to be anywhere but here, with Zayn.

"Do you want to do something else?" Zayn's tone made his meaning more than clear.

Aiden very much did, but his control was tenuous with the moon at her fullest. "I'm not sure I can do anything tonight without biting you. Without bonding you. Knotting you."

A shiver ran through Zayn, and he pinned Aiden with a look. "You don't want to do that? Because I do. I want you to bite me, to bond me. I want to be with you. I want forever with you."

Those words set Aiden's heart racing, the ferocity of his desire for Zayn threatening to unravel what little self-control he retained. He'd never been as driven by his instincts as some shifters, but that night, his wolf was nothing but the primal urge to claim.

The moon's pull intensified every sensation, every emotion. It left him raw with want and need. Zayn's scent reached out to him, heady and beckoning, stroking over his senses, mixing with the moonlight to ignite like wildfire in his veins.

"Are you sure?" Aiden asked, a low growl punctuating the question.

Zayn's eyes searched his, dark with desire and resolve. "More than I've ever been of anything in my life."

The last vestiges of Aiden's restraint vanished, and he gave in to the urges he'd been fighting. He stood and prowled the few steps it took to get to Zayn's chair. Without a word, he tugged Zayn to his feet, the air between them crackling and charged as he leaned down and brought their lips together in a searing kiss.

It had only been a few weeks, but Zayn's body, his touches, his kisses, felt like home, like perfection, like everything Aiden could ever need. He let his wolf take over as he led Zayn into the cabin, the moonlight casting a silvery glow through the large windows as they traded kisses on their way to the bed, reluctantly breaking apart to shed their clothes before tumbling onto the soft blankets.

Aiden ran his hands over Zayn, tracing lines and curves that had etched themselves on his soul, a map he'd studied and memorized as closely as the constellations. He wanted to spend his life exploring it just as thoroughly, finding every spot that'd make Zayn writhe if stroked lightly, every place that'd earn him the sweetest moans when sucked.

Energy hummed inside him, filling him with power and strength. He'd never felt as alive as he did in this moment, his skin tingling with an all-consuming need, with the half-feral instinct to mark, to possess, to give himself to Zayn.

The lust and arousal coming off Zayn was intoxicating, and Aiden feasted on his scent like it alone could sustain him. He trailed his nose down Zayn's chest as he inhaled, his heart pounding, echoing Zayn's thundering pulse.

Zayn arched into Aiden's touch and tangled fingers in his hair. "Fuck, Aiden, *please*," he said, his voice low and rasping.

That was exactly what they'd do, but Aiden wanted to taste him first. He peppered kisses along Zayn's inner thigh, then up his shaft until he was lapping at the precome beading on the tip. Zayn's breath hitched, his stomach clenching as he tried not to buck into Aiden's mouth.

They'd only done this a handful of times, but fuck, Aiden loved it. Loved the taste and feel of Zayn on his tongue, loved the filthy noises that spilled from Zayn's lips, the pleasure he could give his mate this way. Maybe some other night he'd let Zayn fuck his mouth until he came, but tonight, Aiden needed control. He grabbed Zayn's hips and pinned him to the mattress, swallowing him down as far as he could take him. Zayn gasped and cursed with each bob of his head. His arm flailed out, nearly knocking the lamp off the bedside table as he groped around to find the drawer and open it, blindly fumbling inside until he produced a bottle of lube.

Aiden blinked up at him.

"I was hoping," Zayn explained, panting.

How had he gotten that in there without Aiden noticing? It didn't matter; Aiden didn't care. He let Zayn slip from his mouth and grabbed the bottle before settling between his legs again.

This was something else they hadn't done often yet—just a few times each—but he loved it. He didn't think there was anything that he wouldn't love with Zayn.

Lubing up his fingers, he brought them to Zayn's hole, and Zayn spread his legs wider for him, gifting him with the prettiest little whimper as he teased his entrance, then pressed two inside. He'd made Zayn come like this before, working him open as Zayn talked him through it, telling him what he liked, what he wanted Aiden to do to him, how he'd imagined Aiden's fingers inside him whenever he stretched himself before using a toy. And Aiden was nothing if not an excellent student. He knew what Zayn's body was begging for, and he gave it to him as he licked and sucked at his cock.

"I'm good," Zayn said, but Aiden kept going. He maybe wasn't as large as certain toys, but when he claimed Zayn, he wanted to make sure he'd be able to take his knot, and if that meant drawing more cries and pleas from Zayn first, well, that was a sacrifice he was willing to make.

Zayn threaded a hand through his hair and tugged. "*Aiden*, I'm good."

Aiden scissored his fingers once more, getting one last curse, before he crawled up Zayn's body, and Zayn pulled him into a deep, desperate kiss. Aiden's instincts were screaming at him to bury himself inside Zayn, to claim him completely.

He broke the kiss, his breathing heavy. "Ready?"

Zayn gave him a flat look with no heat behind it. "Have been for a while, yeah."

Aiden grinned. "Good." He kissed Zayn again, then

propped himself up on a forearm to watch Zayn's face as he lined himself up.

Despite everything they'd done, they hadn't done this, and Aiden had so many fantasies about how it would go. He nudged against Zayn's entrance, the head of his dick right there, but not pressing in.

"The next time we do this, I want you to ride me like one of your toys. Use me to get yourself off. I've wanted that since I first watched your reviews."

"Next time?" Zayn asked, breathless. "We haven't even gotten to this ti—*oh, fuck, yes.*" He moaned, clutching Aiden as he slowly pushed in.

Nothing had ever felt as good as this. As sinking into Zayn, his tight heat overwhelming in that moment of surrender and completion. Like something inside of Aiden, as ancient as the stars, had finally found its way home after millennia of wandering alone.

A soft gasp escaped Zayn's lips. Their bodies fit together, two halves of a whole, and the little self-control Aiden had left wavered with each breath, each slow thrust, each shared heartbeat. He drank in the sight of the moonlight and shadows dancing over Zayn's skin, and Zayn looked up at him with eyes as dark as the deepest space, hungry and possessive and ready for what came next.

He tilted his head to the side—a plea and an offering, silent permission. Aiden nuzzled into his neck, reveling in his scent.

His fangs dropped, and he scraped them along the juncture of Zayn's neck, eliciting a needy whimper from Zayn, or maybe from himself. He let that tide of desire and instinct wash over him. When he bit down, when his teeth broke skin, the bond that had been waiting for them slid into place, the connection between them unfurling as everything that was Zayn rushed into him, as everything that was him rushed into Zayn.

Zayn knew what Aiden needed; he bit him in return, claiming him as his own. All the sensations and emotions mirrored between them, building in intensity, shivering through them, their desire burning brighter than any star, sweeping them away.

"You have no idea how much I've wanted this," Aiden said, a whispered confession against Zayn's skin, but Zayn was shaking his head. He'd wanted it just as much. Those years of longing swept through their bond.

Aiden's grip tightened, their bodies in perfect sync, their rhythm building to a crescendo that swirled through them like a cosmic storm. Every cell, every particle of their beings, seemed connected.

Ecstasy coursed through them as Aiden's knot began to swell. Zayn groaned, his eyes locking on Aiden's, and Aiden sensed everything he was experiencing: the glorious feeling of being stretched open farther and farther, the need to be filled impossibly full, all combining with the demanding throb of his knot, the hot clench of Zayn's heat around him. It entwined until he could no longer separate what came from him and what came from Zayn.

He slammed into Zayn a final time, his knot fully expanding, tying them together. Zayn shuddered against him as their orgasms hit. He spilled between them, and Aiden released deep inside him, leaving them trembling and panting, clinging to each other as they rode out the aftershocks.

They lay naked, limbs intertwined, bodies still connected. The heat of their passion lingered, and they relished its warm glow as the cool air in the room caressed their sweat-damp skin, slowly bringing them back to Earth.

Aiden's wolf rumbled a low, contented sound, secure in the knowledge that Zayn was theirs, that they were Zayn's in return. The bond they shared was transcendent, their scents mingling and merging into something beyond perfection.

Zayn huffed out a shaky laugh. "So this is level-ten inflation. I think I might have to dock a star from Mr. Knotz because he doesn't begin to compare."

Aiden couldn't help but smile, grinding into Zayn and earning a choked-off moan. "Does that mean I get five stars?"

"There are not enough stars in the universe for what you deserve."

"Same." Aiden buried his face in Zayn's neck and breathed him in. "You smell so good after you come. When I'd go on a full-moon run after you started reviewing toys, I knew I'd come home to the scent of your pleasure filling the apartment. I knew what you'd be doing while I was gone. It was torture. But none of those times were a fraction as perfect as you smell right now—my scent covering you, my knot stretching you, my come inside you."

Zayn shivered, pulling him closer, and Aiden ground into him again, dragging ragged moans out of Zayn with every movement of his hips, but he kept his rhythm slow. There was no hurry; they had all the time in the world.

In a few months, they'd graduate, and then they'd go to grad school together; Aiden felt that with a certainty deep in his soul. They'd continue their studies together, be ridiculously stressed together as they wrote their theses, celebrate as they got their doctorates together. They'd discover planets and galaxies. Their names would be written in the stars so that, for the rest of human history, people would look up into the night sky and know them and their love.

But even if that didn't happen, this was more than enough. Their bond was as infinite as the universe that stretched out around them with its vast, glittering beauty —glorious and eternal.

They had each other, and that would always be enough.

FOURTEEN

THEN

October, Junior Year

The world was pleasantly fuzzy as Zayn swayed his way home. He wasn't drunk, not completely, but he was also far enough from sober that he was glad he could walk to his apartment.

One of the things that had surprised him the most about college was how wild the Astronomy Club's parties got.

When he opened the apartment door, he blinked owlishly to find Aiden sitting in their living room. Aiden had been gone the night before—it'd been a full moon, after all—and he hadn't returned by the time Zayn had left for the day.

Zayn wandered over to the couch and plopped down on it, grinning at Aiden. "You're here. But of course you'd be here. Unlike last night, when you weren't here, you know? But it's okay. You were doing your thing."

"My thing?" The question came out like a squeak.

Zayn nodded solemnly. "The moonlit orgies. I figured it out. But I understand it's a secret."

Aiden looked beyond confused. "I'm not having moonlit orgies. Or any orgies."

"Right. Uh-huh." Zayn winked at him. "But I won't tell anyone. I'm very good at keeping secrets. I mean, I've been keeping a secret from you for so long. You don't even know that I—" Zayn cut himself off, his brain screeching to a halt when he realized what he was about to say.

Oh, shit. Abort. Not good.

He couldn't do this. Aiden was still out of his league, as evidenced by his monthly moonlit orgies. Zayn didn't want to mess up their friendship by confessing *that*.

His mind flailed around frantically as he tried to come up with a way to finish his sentence without incriminating himself. He blurted out the first thing that popped into his head. "I have a site where I review sex toys."

Zayn winced. Admitting that wasn't much better. It might have been worse.

"What?" Aiden asked, his voice cracking on the word.

Cringing, Zayn said, "Uh, yeah. In May, I started a blog to post reviews of various toys. I called it InZayn Reviews. Like insane, but also, *in Zayn*. And um, a couple of months ago, I began to... post video reviews."

"Videos of you talking about the toys?"

"Um. Videos of me *using* the toys. For my reviews."

"Oh. *Oh*." Aiden stared at him with wide eyes. "You put videos of yourself doing that on the internet?"

Zayn shook his head. "No. Well, yes, but they're behind a paywall."

"A paywall. Oh. That's... smart." Aiden swallowed.

"Yeah, my site has been getting pretty popular. I'm making

good money from it now, and it's kind of fun. It was a little strange at first to film myself, but once I got used to it, I started to enjoy it. Like, *really* enjoy it, and other people like it too."

Zayn let out a relieved exhale. It felt better to have that off his chest. He hadn't told anyone, and not telling Aiden had been driving him crazy. He told Aiden everything.

Okay, *almost* everything. There was one secret he'd be keeping to himself for sure, but he was happy he didn't need to hide this anymore. He'd be able to talk about it to Aiden now; he wouldn't have to lie about the fact that he was suddenly not broke, or invent any more lame excuses for what was in all the discreet packages he'd been receiving.

"I... I'm glad you're... enjoying yourself." Aiden looked flustered, a hint of heat in his cheeks.

Maybe Zayn was imagining it, but he swore Aiden's breathing was faster. Though that was probably the alcohol talking, impairing his judgment. It was certainly responsible for his next question, something he never would have asked if he were entirely sober.

"Do you want to see my site?" Zayn felt foolishly hopeful as he searched Aiden's face, but Aiden quickly shook his head.

"Oh, no. We're... friends. It'd be weird, right?"

Zayn held back a wince. "Right. Friends wouldn't watch each other do that."

"Well," Aiden said, standing up and looking around the room like he'd never seen it before. His eyes locked on the door to his bedroom. "It's late. I should... Yeah, I should go to bed." He took a few steps in that direction, froze, then spun around and grabbed his laptop before making a beeline to his room.

Aiden's door shut with a decisive click, and Zayn stared at it for a long moment.

Of course Aiden wouldn't want to watch his reviews. That was fine. Other people did, and maybe someday, Zayn would find someone even half as attractive as Aiden. Stranger things had happened. And until then, he had plenty of toys to review. Eventually he had to come across one that deserved five stars.

FIFTEEN

Aiden's phone buzzed repeatedly, and he knew who it would be before he checked it. He'd gotten a dozen similar messages as he and Zayn had driven to Los Angeles.

BRAM

Are you there yet?

Has he signed it?

Have you seen anyone?

AIDEN

Yes, he's in there now, and no.

He swore Bram was more excited about this contract than Zayn. It wouldn't have surprised him if Bram had tried to stow away in their car to get into MateHub's headquarters. He'd even been the one to find the perfect agent to help Zayn negotiate his contract—a vampire named Adrian who represented MateHub's only human star, Hunter Savage.

Zayn was signing on to film a few reviews for MateHub,

with the potential to extend the contract if his videos went over well. He'd still be filming his usual reviews for his human viewers, but now he and Aiden would occasionally drive to LA for Zayn to review MateHub's merch in a more professional setting, with better cameras and lighting.

MateHub had made it clear Zayn would never be allowed to do more than that. He wouldn't be considered an official MateHub star and wouldn't do scenes for them. His bond with Aiden disqualified him from those kinds of contracts—a fact that neither Aiden nor Zayn was particularly distraught over.

BRAM

Next time you go, you need to take me with you.

Please take me with you?

AIDEN

We aren't bringing you with us so you can loiter in the halls, hoping you run into Richard Knotz.

BRAM

It doesn't have to be Richard. I've got a whole list.

Aiden snorted. He had no doubt Bram did.

BRAM

OOH. Do you think he'll get invited to the year-end award show?

Can I go with him as his plus one if he does?

AIDEN

Can you be my mate's plus one to a porn award show?

Let me think about that.

Ummm...

NO.

But if it does happen, we'll try to get you a ticket too. How about that?

BRAM

Have I ever told you that you're my best friend? The absolute bestest of best?

The forum guys would be so jealous.

Aiden was about to respond, but the door to the meeting room opened, and Zayn, his agent, and a few representatives from MateHub stepped out. Zayn was grinning, his presence in Aiden's mind a pleased warmth, and when he looked and felt this happy, it was impossible not to smile in return.

"All set?" Aiden asked, and Zayn nodded.

"The contract's signed, and they said they'd give us a tour if we're interested."

"Might as well." How many times did one get the chance to tour a porn studio? Plus, he was curious to see where Zayn would be filming.

Zayn's agent and a MateHub representative led them through the building, wandering through the production offices and past the editing rooms. The props department had Aiden's eyebrows climbing, and wardrobe seemed to consist mainly of outfits that required some serious suspension of disbelief. Either that, or he was ordering from the wrong pizza places, because a delivery driver had never once shown up in a sheer crop top with "Craving a good topping? Call Hot and Ready Pizza" written in glitter on the front.

Their next stop was one of the sets. The moment they stepped inside, Aiden's breath was stolen by the sight, and Zayn's shock reverberated through their bond.

Illusions had transformed the space into a massive Greek temple with rows of columns stretching into the distance. The scent of magic lingered in the air, making Aiden's nose itch.

The crew bustled about, preparing for the scene. They adjusted lights and positioned the cameras surrounding an altar fit for worshiping a god.

"Um," Zayn said, a concerned expression on his face.

His agent chuckled, shaking his head. "They'll arrange a much smaller set for your reviews. They only do things like this for their biggest stars."

"I'd say don't let Richard hear that, but unlike other parts of his anatomy, I don't think his head can swell any bigger than it already is," a voice said behind them, and they spun around to find Tristan standing there. He looked Aiden and Zayn over with a disinterested gaze. "I take it I can stop searching for salt."

Aiden grinned. "Yeah. No salt needed."

"Salt?" Zayn asked.

"I'll explain later."

"So," Tristan said, "are you sticking around for the filming? I can guarantee you'll see a colossal dick. His penis is marginally larger than average too."

"Ah..." Aiden didn't know how to respond to that. Watching MateHub was one thing, but he wasn't sure he wanted to watch live porn for anything other than Zayn's reviews.

"As nice as a giant dick can be," Zayn said, "I think we're good."

Tristan shrugged. "Suit yourself." He turned to leave.

"Thank you," Aiden called after him.

"No idea what you're talking about. Salt is just so scarce these days." He waved a dismissive hand and walked away.

"Yeah, you're definitely explaining that later." Zayn's brow furrowed as he tried to figure out how salt could be difficult to come by. Aiden would explain, but before that, they had a tour to finish.

After they were done, a photographer took pictures of Zayn for the announcement and his profile on the site. She even snapped a few of them together. That was followed by a brief interview, and then they were free to go. They'd be back for Zayn to film his reviews, but they had things to do before then.

At the top of their list was driving up to Aiden's pack so Zayn could meet them. Aiden usually managed the trip in two grueling days, but they'd be taking it at a more leisurely pace. They had four stops planned along the way, all perfect for nighttime observations, if they could unwrap themselves from each other for long enough to do that.

It'd be the first of many times they'd make this trip together, since they'd be staying in California for grad school, something they'd confirmed when their acceptance emails had arrived in their inboxes the week before.

As they left MateHub's headquarters, Zayn glanced at him with a soft smile that made Aiden's heart skip a beat. They got into their car, and Aiden pulled out onto the busy streets of LA.

The sun was bright and high in the sky, casting a warm golden glow over the city as they headed toward the open road. Zayn's hand rested gently on his thigh, and contentment permeated their bond.

They drove until they'd left the noise and chaos and light pollution far behind them. The initial blush of civil twilight darkened the sky, and Venus's brilliant white pierced through the remnants of the day, soon joined by Sirius, Capella, Orion's Betelgeuse and Rigel, and, eventually, countless more.

This was the beginning of their journey, and it felt like gazing into the vast expanse of the night sky, knowing endless wonders awaited them among the stars. The road stretched out ahead, beckoning them to explore, and with Zayn by his side, Aiden had every intention of doing exactly that.

BREAKING NEWS: Zayn from InZayn Reviews signs contract to review for MateHub!

FabulousFoxxx:
The crossover we deserve!

KnottyWolf69:
Wait. Does this mean we get to see him review Richard's merch after all?

queenbanana:
But he's human. How did he find out about the supernatural?

FabulousFoxxx:
His profile is already up. Go check it out. He's mated to a wolf shifter. There's even a picture.

KnottyWolf69:
Damn, that mating bite looks FRESH. I bet they're still in the fucking like bunnies stage.

lumberjacklover:
Ooh, gotta love that possessive arm his mate has wrapped around his waist.

queenbanana:
Is Mr. InZayn's name listed anywhere? We need a pairing name for them.

BramStroker:

You didn't hear it from me, but his mate's name is Aiden. They've been pining after each other for literally years and finally got their shit together.

readyorknot:

Zayn and Aiden? That's cute. What about Zayden?

HuntMeDown:

Clearly it should be AtoZ.

MagicalHWood:

Or not. Maybe you shouldn't be allowed to name anything.

readyorknot:

Whatever we call them, can they do a scene together? Zayn should review Aiden's dick for us. Or Aiden could help him test out some of the MateHub partner merch.

FabulousFoxxx:

There's no way MateHub will go for that. Reviews are one thing, but they won't hire a true-bonded couple to do scenes for them.

lumberjacklover:

Even if he only does solo reviews, it'll be fun to see what he thinks. After those crappy human toys, MateHub's merch will be an easy five stars.

HuntMeDown:

This is going to end with me buying everything he reviews, isn't it? My wallet is going to hate me.

KnottyWolf69:

Yep! But what can you do? Not watch? Yeah right.

BramStroker:

I can't believe we're getting this news today, and tomorrow we'll get an announcement about Richard Knotz's next bonding contract!

MagicalHWood:

I cannot wait for all the hot scenes Richard will give us this time.

readyorknot:

100%! See you guys in the forums!

End of Five Star Review

Thank you for reading!

BRAM

OOH. Do you think he'll get invited to the year-end award show?

Can I go with him as his plus one if he does?

Sign up for my mailing list to receive bonus scenes from this novella, including Zayn and Aiden bringing Bram to the MateHub Awards and Aiden checking out Zayn's site for the first time. You'll also get regular updates on my upcoming releases and an occasional free short story.

MATEHUB: LEGEND

Want to meet the shifter behind the merch? Read Richard Knotz's story in *MateHub: Legend*.

The contract was simple: three months, seven scenes, zero feelings. Following it was not.

In the world of supernatural adult entertainment, Richard Knotz is a legend, and knotting scenes are his brand. No human could ever threaten to tear his empire to the ground, no matter how tempting that human smells.

Available now on Amazon and in Kindle Unlimited.

ELEMENTAL BONDS

Want to meet Aiden's pack? Check out *Elemental Bonds*.

Accidental Bonds (Elemental Bonds Book One)

Victor Mills may detest magic, but the mage he's hired to protect his pack smells like everything his wolf has ever wanted. As an insidious rot creeps through his territory, he must learn to trust the mage and the growing bond between them. If he fails, his pack will pay the ultimate price.

Available now on Amazon and in Kindle Unlimited.

Impulsive Connections (Elemental Bonds Book Two)

After a run-in with a malicious spirit leaves Kade Mills reluctantly bonded to a bookish mage, he struggles to resist the heady pull of their unwanted connection. But he soon discovers that bond could be the key to saving everything he holds dear… and it might not be as unwelcome as he thought.

Available now on Amazon and in Kindle Unlimited.

Unexpected Alliances (Elemental Bonds Book Three)

Coming soon.

ACKNOWLEDGMENTS

This novella is a spinoff of a spinoff. A joke in my first novel, *Accidental Bonds*, spawned *MateHub: Legend*, and then *MateHub* spawned this. Because obviously if my paranormal porn stars have merch, someone needs to be using it. A year ago, if you'd told me I'd be researching astrophysics so I could write a story about a knotting dildo bringing two oblivious idiots together... Well, I probably would have believed you about everything except the astrophysics.

I'd like to thank my beta reader, Amy Pittel, for her wonderful feedback on this and for putting me in touch with an astronomer. This novella would not be the same without her.

My deepest gratitude goes to Christian Ready of Towson University and the creator of the Launch Pad Astronomy YouTube channel. He very kindly checked my astronomy homework for this. Any additional errors in the science are entirely my own.

Next, I want to thank Kate Wood for editing this book. She does an amazing job at catching all the typos I miss.

I also want to say how much I appreciate Kate Munro for encouraging me to write this rather crazy story and for helping me organize the 2023 Debut M/M Author Event for which it was written.

And a special thank you to Laura Lee, Juliana, Leigh, and Laurie for appearing in the MateHub forums for this novella. To the rest of my newsletter subscribers who entered for a chance to have a cameo, I hope you'll sign up again for the next *MateHub* book, which will have more cameo slots available. I love that you all are willing to let me put you in the fan forums, and the usernames you submit amuse the hell out of me.

Finally, thank you, dear reader! I hope you enjoyed this novella. If you're a new-to-me reader, I hope you'll consider checking out my other books. And whether you're a new or returning reader, I look forward to sharing more stories with you in the future.

If you could spare a moment to leave a review of *Five Star Review* on Amazon or a site such as Goodreads or Book-Bub, it would mean the world to me. Reviews help indie authors gain visibility and reach more readers, and I appreciate each one, no matter how long or short.

Please feel free to reach out to me on any of the social media sites listed on my About the Author page. I'd love to hear from you.

Thank you again, and happy reading!

ABOUT THE AUTHOR

Marie Reynard is an American in Japan, teaching English by day and writing M/M paranormal romance by night. Her steamy, snarky stories will take you from first kiss to forever with a few Fs in between—including found family, flirty banter, fake dating, and a fair amount of fu...n. Check out her website for more information on her books, and join her mailing list to get a free story or two and be the first to know about upcoming releases!

Website - https://www.mariereynard.com/
Newsletter - http://subscribepage.io/y7lohL
Facebook Group - https://facebook.com/groups/
mariereynardsden/

facebook.com/authormariereynard

tiktok.com/@marie_reynard

x.com/marie_reynard

instagram.com/marie__reynard

amazon.com/author/mariereynard

goodreads.com/mariereynard

bookbub.com/profile/marie-reynard